A SEPARATE SEASON

By

Paul D. Ellner

ISBN: 0-75962-714-2

This book is printed on acid free paper.

1stBooks - rev. 5/1/01

To everything there is a season, and a time to every purpose under heaven:

Ecclesiastes 3:1

For Connie, with love

ACKNOWLEDGEMENTS

I am very grateful for the help I received in writing this story. I would like to thank Carol Andersen, Des Moines; Nicholas F. Bellantoni, Connecticut State Archeologist; Nona Bloomer, Historical Room Librarian, Guilford Free Library; Ernst Burnham, Esquire, Clinton; Richard Carlton, M.D., psychiatrist; Edward Doran, numismatist; Professor Robert Ellickson, Yale Law School; Conrad Ellner, M.D., psychiatrist; David Ellner, paramedic; Jonathan Ellner; Joel Helander, Historian and Probate Judge, Guilford; Roger Kinderman, Manager, Hammonasset State Park; Nancy Lex, Branch Manager, Citibank; Warren Lord, Archivist, Madison; Yvonne Lue, Ph.D.; Michael McBride, Whitfield House Museum, Guilford; Rev. Michael Moran, Pastor, First Congregational Church, New Milford; Diane Myers; Marcia Oliver; and Dave Poirier, Staff Archeologist, Connecticut Historical Commission. All gave generously of their time and special knowledge.

Shortly after crossing the Hammonasset River, a tourist driving East on the Boston Post Road, will enter the small town of Clinton, Connecticut. At the corner of Highland Drive the visitor will see a sign “Rowland Colonial Farm, 2 miles.” Should time and curiosity tempt him or her to see the farm, the paved road will become a dirt one in less than half a mile and end at a small wooden farmhouse and barn. If it is summer or early fall, there will be stands of corn, wheat, rye and flax in the fields behind the barn, a cow and a few sheep in a nearby meadow. The house has only two rooms; the main room with a fireplace, a wooden table and chairs and a small adjoining bedroom. Attached to the wall over the fireplace is a bronze plaque with the curious inscription “In memory of Daniel Rowland, born 1732 died 1999, aged 38.”

CHAPTER 1

Guilford, Connecticut, 1790

Daniel did not know that this day was to be his last in this life. He awoke before dawn as he usually did and remained still for a few moments, transitioning from sleep to wakefulness. He had been dreaming; something about a small child. He tried to remember but already the dream was fleeting. Elizabeth lay on her side close to him, her warm body damp from perspiration. He quietly rolled out of the bed taking care not to disturb her and pulled on his clothes. He lit a candle in a lamp and walked out to the moist darkness of the yard.

The stars were still visible and the damp, cool air was redolent with the mingled odors of hay and clover, urine and manure. Buttercup was waiting for him at the edge of the field and he led her into the barn. He sat on a low stool and rested his forehead against her warm flank as he pulled on her teats, and made the rich, white fluid to spurt into the pail with a musical sound.

There should be children to drink this milk, he thought. There was a little one but now she's gone. This farm...Elizabeth, and I need children to lift the loneliness of the silent days and nights.

The sky was already light when he turned the cow out to the meadow and checked to see that the six sheep were all there. Nell ambled over to greet him with a soft whinny and he gave her an apple. Daniel loved horses.

You are very important to us, old girl, he thought as he patted her neck. You pull the plow, drag logs, draw the wagon and sometimes even serve me as a mount.

Daniel was the sole surviving offspring of Isaac Rowland. Isaac, together with a company of men from Guilford, had marched all the way to Albany, New York and then on to Vermont to fight the French at Lake Champlain in 1759. When

Isaac returned from the war the grateful town fathers granted him, and each of his fellow soldiers, eighteen acres of good farm land in the Hammonasset meadows. Daniel's mother died when he was seven; she did not survive her second pregnancy and the child was stillborn.

As a lad, Daniel helped his father with the farm. At sixteen he started attending the school at Flag Marsh. The school was ten miles from the farm so Daniel stayed with a family on nearby Moose Hill. He returned home on Saturdays, accompanied his father to church on Sunday and walked back to school on Monday. He was a bright student, eager and quick to learn but the schoolmaster often had to chastise him for his impatience with some of his slower schoolmates. He attended school for two months each year for the next four years. Isaac died in 1779 leaving Daniel the farm and a small amount of money.

Daniel had a habit of repeatedly drumming his fingers, one at a time in turn on his body or on a table, starting with his little finger as if playing a musical instrument. He was thorough and conscientious in his work but always impatient to get on with it. A quiet young man, reticent with strangers, but affable enough with friends and neighbors, he was well regarded in Guilford as an honest and industrious farmer. His gray eyes looked keenly at whatever he encountered, reflecting the intelligence and kindness within.

He met Elizabeth at church. He was thirty, she was eighteen; a slim, pretty girl with blond hair and a face unmarked by the pox. He sat behind her for several Sundays before he was able to find a plausible reason to start a conversation with her after the long service was over. His prayer was answered by a sudden gust that blew her bonnet off as she and her parents walked from the meeting-house. He rushed to retrieve it as it rolled along the muddy ground.

"Now truly, Miss, I presume this bonnet must belong to you."

"Indeed, sir, I thank you." Her blue eyes twinkled. "I am sure no one has ever chased this bonnet so well." Daniel's ruddy face turned a deeper shade of crimson.

"Now, Elizabeth..." her father admonished, seeing Daniel's embarrassment.

"If it is not an indecorum," Daniel managed to say, "I would fain call on your daughter." Her father smiled and nodded his assent.

Her parents favored the relationship and they were married after a two-year courtship. A year later their cup of happiness overflowed with the birth of Abigail, a beautiful child that they both adored. The child was only a year old when she developed croup and despite everything the distraught parents could do, the little girl died. They buried her behind the house.

He and Elizabeth traveled the six and a half miles into town almost every Sunday to attend divine services at the meeting-house in Guilford. Their farm was productive, with Indian corn, wheat, rye, flax and apples as their main crops and a few sheep, chickens, the horse and their cow as the livestock. Elizabeth grew peas, beans, cabbages, parsnips and turnips in her garden. She baked bread from corn meal and rye flour, made cider and vinegar from their Bristow apples, linen homespun cloth from the flax, and the wool from the sheep became shirts and stockings.

The Revolution started in 1775. Most of the folks in Guilford were patriotic and even those few loyal to King George felt that the newly imposed taxes were grossly unfair. There was little major fighting in Connecticut; a few skirmishes in Stonington, New Haven and New London and the British were driven from Danbury by colonial troops led by Captain Benedict Arnold.

In Guilford, the men built a guardhouse on the coast and maintained a nightly watch of twenty-four men. Daniel took his turn on the watch but otherwise he stayed on the farm with his father. Isaac was ailing and Daniel was needed to maintain the farm.

Daniel's life became dull after the death of their child. He missed the weight of her on his shoulder, her sweet smell and her childish sounds. He and Elizabeth tried to comfort each other with prayer but he had an ache in his chest whenever he thought of the baby. He welcomed each day's labor as a diversion from his sorrow and he observed that Elizabeth seemed to be doing the same thing by busying herself with her chores. In the evening they both sat quietly; Daniel read and Elizabeth sewed or spun until the twilight faded to darkness and the single candle barely lit the small room. In bed they often clung to each other silently, sometimes without making love, and fell asleep in each other's arms.

*

The August sun rose in a cloudless sky, heralded by the fanfare of a trumpeting rooster and the cawing of a squadron of crows passing overhead. The smell of new mown hay drifted in through the open window and a few flies began to buzz around the small room. Elizabeth became aware of the clucking of hens. She opened her eyes and slowly stretched. A wave of nausea came over her and she lay quietly until it passed. She contemplated the bare walls, the small chest of drawers and the empty rocking cradle resting in one corner.

Now I am certain, she thought. I missed my last monthly and my breasts have grown heavier. I am carrying a child. I must tell Daniel.

The sickness soon left her and she rose, put on a linen underdress and a calico gown and went into the main room to prepare breakfast for Daniel. She was putting warm johnnycake and a mug of milk on the table when he walked in.

"Good morning, Elizabeth. It looks like another hot day."

"Pray sit down, " she said with a smile. "I have some news for you."

"I trust it is not ill news."

"Nay, I deem it good news." She walked behind his chair and placed her hands on his shoulders.

"I am carrying a child." He rose and took her in his arms.

"Of a certainty?"

"Verily," She blushed and looked away. "My monthly flow was due three weeks ago." His face lit up.

"Now truly that is the best of news. Let us go tell little Abigail that she will soon have a brother or a sister."

They walked to the small grave behind the house. Daniel picked a bunch of wildflowers and placed them in front of the wooden marker. Together they knelt in silence for a few minutes and then rose, hand in hand to return to the house.

"Daniel, could you mayhap go to the marsh and dig some clams? I had a fancy to make some chowder." He smiled assent and went to harness Nell to the wagon.

"Will you come?" he called.

"Nay, the garden wants weeding and the wretched beetles are devouring the cabbages."

"Farewell, then. I will return before dark."

She waved as the wagon pulled away.

He is so pleased, she thought. We need this child.

Daniel drove along the Totoket Path that would take him to the mouth of the West River where the best clams and oysters were to be found, a distance of some seven miles. The path forded Horse Brook, and the Neck and East Rivers. Past the old Griswold House, he turned on to a path that led to the beach. The weather was beginning to cloud up and the air had become hot and humid. By the time he reached Turkey Point, the sky had darkened and there was a warm, brisk wind blowing in from the Sound. He left his shoes in the wagon, tied Nell to a tree and took a sack for the clams. He walked along the beach towards Leete's Island, whistling tunelessly. The tide was out and finding the shellfish was easy.

He had only dug a few clams when he saw flashes of lightning and heard the first cannonading of thunder. He tried to dig and walk faster, hoping to find enough clams before the storm broke. His attention was drawn to a peculiar cloud that was forming about a mile offshore. It was low over the water, very black with green fringes and frequent flashes of lightning. The cloud was unlike anything he had ever seen and it moved toward the beach at a rapid rate, appearing to roll over the water.

I dare not wait here for yonder storm to catch me, he thought and he began to run. He was about five hundred yards from the wagon when the cloud reached the beach and swept over him. He was suddenly encompassed by darkness. He could not even see the sand at his feet and he was forced to stop running and stand still. It was like being shut in a dark closet. All the hairs on his body stood out. It was very hot and moist and he could hardly breathe. Daniel was frightened. A humming sound grew louder and higher pitched and his whole body was enveloped with a greenish glow. Suddenly there was a tremendous bolt of lightning that seemed to strike him and he knew no more.

*

Elizabeth waited for Daniel through the night. After several hours the storm passed but he failed to return. At first light she walked the few miles to their nearest neighbor who agreed to take her in his wagon to look for Daniel. They found Daniel's wagon with Nell still tied up. His shoes were in the wagon but there was no sign of him. Later, they rounded up a small group of town folk to help. They searched the marsh and the beach for several days but found nothing. The storm had washed away any footprints that Daniel might have left. They assumed that in some inexplicable way he had been washed out to sea, but his body was never recovered.

*

Elizabeth was heartbroken. She spent a few days with her parents in town where the minister and some friends paid condolence calls but she insisted on returning to the farm. She remained there and continued the daily chores until she felt the time was at hand for the baby. She arranged with a neighbor to care for the livestock during her absence; harnessed Nell to the wagon and drove to her parent's house in town. A week later she went into labor and delivered a healthy boy. She named him Noah. Elizabeth stayed with her parents for a month and then, despite their advice, she returned to the farm with her son. The neighboring farmer harvested her crops and sheared the sheep; Elizabeth cared for Noah, milked the cow, fed the chickens, and tended her garden.

Her parents visited almost every week and tried to persuade her to sell the farm and to live in town with them where life would be easier, but she was determined to remain.

"This is our Rowland farm," she insisted, "and so it shall remain. That is what Daniel would have wished."

CHAPTER 2

Hamden, Connecticut, 1998

Joseph finished the last morsel of his bacon and eggs, and leaned back in his chair. He drank some coffee and briefly regarded the bird activity at the feeder outside the window. He felt very calm and contented.

"You know, Lin," he told his wife, "this is the first Saturday I've had off since the end of the semester. Why don't we all do something?" Linda looked up from the newspaper she was reading.

"Sounds like a good idea. What did you have in mind?"

"Maybe we could have a picnic. Drive to the Westwood Hiking Trail over in Guilford, walk to the beach and picnic there. I'll ask the kids."

Joseph Pellegrini, Ph.D., was a third generation Italian-American. Almost six feet tall, with a thickening waist and a bald spot on the crown of his head surrounded by black hair he had the appearance of a tall monk.

Joseph was interested in history since childhood. He read every book he could lay his hands on that dealt with history. At City College in New York he majored in History and entered graduate school at the University of Connecticut. His field of specialization was the American colonial period.

He and Linda met at the UConn Student Union. She planned to be a teacher. They began dating regularly, often going to The Creamery for ice cream or the Clark House for a hamburger. They received their degrees at the same commencement exercise; an M.A. for her and a Ph.D. for him. Two weeks later they married.

Joseph accepted a position as instructor in the History Department of Quinnipiac College in Hamden. They bought a home in Hamden where they raised their children. Linda taught English at Hamden High School.

*

Nick and Cathy were on the couch in the den watching cartoons on TV and sharing a bag of tortilla chips. Both children wore faded jeans, dirty white sneakers, and sweatshirts. Joseph had to stand directly in front of the TV to get their attention.

"Would you guys like to go on a picnic?"

"Where?" Cathy asked. At fourteen, she demanded to know the details of everything.

"Mom and I thought we might hike the Westwood Trail to the beach in Guilford, and..." Nick leaped from the couch, causing his New York Yankee baseball cap to fall off his head.

"Can I drive, Dad? You promised you'd take me out for practice." Nick was preparing to take his driving test, having turned sixteen a month ago.

"Well, we'll see."

They traveled east on the Interstate with Nick at the wheel, Linda and Cathy in the back. Nick wore his baseball cap backwards and concentrated intently on his driving. Joseph tried to appear relaxed. They turned off I-95 at the Guilford Exit, passed Bishop's Apple Orchard, and then turned on to Dunk Rock Road that led to the trail.

Nick and Cathy carried the cooler and walked ahead. Linda and Joseph followed with blankets and a jug of lemonade. The trail wound through the marsh toward the beach. As they neared the beach, the trail turned, so that they lost sight of the children. Moments later they heard Cathy scream. Nick was yelling, "Dad, Dad!"

Joseph and Linda dropped their burdens and raced ahead. Both children were standing on the trail pointing excitedly to something on the ground. As Joseph and Linda came up to them, they could see it was the body of a man.

He lay face down with his arms at his sides. His eyes were closed. Joseph knelt to examine him. The man was breathing but unconscious. There did not appear to be any obvious wound.

Joseph carefully rolled the man over. He was young, muscular, dressed in a white vest and close fitting pants that ended at the knees. He wore no shoes. A colonial style three-cornered hat lay on the ground nearby.

"Is he dead?" Cathy asked, clinging to her mother's hand.

"No, he's breathing," Joseph said, "but he's sick or hurt."

"We need to get some help, Joe," Linda said. "I'll call 911 with the car phone." She hurried away.

"Why is he dressed like that, Dad?" Nick asked.

"Maybe he's an actor in a play or something," Joseph told him.

Twenty minutes later, Linda returned leading two paramedics carrying a stretcher. They examined the prostrate figure.

"I don't smell any alcohol on him," one of the paramedics said. "Let's get him to the hospital."

"Where are you going to take him?" Joseph asked.

"Yale-New Haven."

"I'm going to go with them," Joseph told Linda. "I want to learn more about this. I'll see you guys at home."

He followed the paramedics carrying the inert figure back to the ambulance and with lights flashing and siren howling, they raced toward New Haven.

CHAPTER 3

The ambulance bearing Joseph and the unconscious Daniel backed into the receiving bay at Yale-New Haven Hospital. The paramedics wheeled the stretcher into the Emergency Room where the triage nurse met them. Joseph stood nearby.

"What's the story on this one?" she demanded.

"He was found unconscious in a marsh in Guilford by this gentleman. No obvious wounds or bleeding. Pulse, respiration and blood pressure seem O.K. We drew a blood sample and started a Coma Cocktail." An IV containing dextrose, thiamine and Narcan, an antidote for narcotics, was dripping into Daniel's vein.

"O.K., put him in that cubicle."

Daniel was transferred to a bed in a small booth separated from the corridor by curtains. Joseph watched as one of the emergency room physicians began to examine Daniel.

Gradually, as if from a great distance, Daniel became aware of unfamiliar voices.

"Get me a chem screen, blood alcohol and a tox panel, skull films and..." The voice trailed off.

Slowly, the memories began to came back. The beach...he was digging clams for Elizabeth...the storm...the black cloud. Daniel opened his eyes. At first, everything was blurred. He was in an unfamiliar place. His vision began to clear and he discerned a man standing over him. The man wore a white coat and had tubes coming out of his ears. The tubes were touching Daniel's chest. Another man, wearing strange clothes, stood at the foot of the bed.

"I think he's waking up."

Daniel tried to sit up but the man in the white coat gently pushed him back down.

"Easy does it. Just stay lying down for a little while."

Easy does it? What does that mean? He looked around. There was a tube running into his arm dripping water from some kind of a bag. What were they doing to him? Who were they? Where was he? What was happening? He struggled wildly to get up, but the man in white restrained him.

"Get me some Haldol!" the man in white shouted. A black nurse brought something with a needle and stuck it into Daniel's arm.

Daniel felt panic overwhelming him. He continued to struggle and thrash around but the man in white was leaning on his chest.

They are trying to kill me!

"Please!" he screamed. "Please spare me, I beseech you!"

Then a ringing in his ears, the room began to spin, and darkness overcame him.

*

When Daniel woke again he was in bed in a larger room. Light came from some kind of lamp in the ceiling; daylight from a window. His wrists were tied to the bed. The man in the strange garments approached his bed and smiled at him.

"How are you feeling?" Joseph asked.

"Indeed sir, I am most wretched. Pray tell me where this place is?"

"We're in the Yale-New Haven Hospital."

"Hospital? What is a hospital? And why am I bound?"

"A hospital is a place for taking care of sick people," Joseph told him. "And you were pretty wild in the Emergency Room."

"Pretty wild?" Daniel said. "Your speech is strange."

A black nurse entered the room and attempted to take his temperature with a thermometer that she placed in his ear. Daniel moved his head from side to side.

"Lie still now, this won't hurt you," she ordered.

"Is this your slave or indentured servant, sir? Pray tell her to leave me."

"Can he be untied?" Joseph asked.

"It's O.K. with us as long as he doesn't get violent."

The nurse left and Joseph released Daniel from the restraints.

"Truly sir, I am most grateful to you. May I ask your name?"

"Joseph. Joseph Pellegrini. You can call me Joe."

"An unusual name, Joe. And your speech is strange. Are you a foreigner?"

"No, I'm from Hamden. What's *your* name, and where do you live?"

"My name is Daniel Rowland. I live on my farm in Guilford where my poor wife Elizabeth must surely be distraught waiting for my return. What day is this?"

"It's Friday, the twelfth of June."

"Now truly, friend Joe, that cannot be. When I left my farm this noon it was the ninth of August. Is there a chamber pot beneath the bed? I need to..."

"Use the bathroom, Daniel. That door there." Daniel got out of bed a little unsteadily. He had on a hospital gown. He opened the bathroom door and was stunned by the array of porcelain and plumbing.

"Upon my word! What is all this?"

Joseph pointed to the toilet. "Use that."

While Daniel was in the bathroom, Joseph examined the clothes that were on a chair. The vest was of a material that seemed to be linen; the pants had no pockets and were of similar material. There was a pair of short homespun drawers. All appeared to be hand sewn; there were no labels. Tied to the leather belt was a piece of cloth containing two copper coins. They bore the bust of a man wearing a laurel wreath and the words: AUCTORI:CONNEC. The other side of the coins showed the figure of a woman holding a long staff in one hand and an olive branch in the other, with the words: INDE:ET.LIB: 1785. Joseph slipped the coins into his pocket.

Daniel called out from the bathroom, "Sir, this great role of paper..."

"Please use it!" Joseph responded.

Daniel emerged from the bathroom. He had not flushed. Joseph showed him how to flush and to use the sink.

"This water, sir, where does it come from? Where does it go?" Before Joseph could explain there was a knock at the door. A young doctor entered and addressed Daniel.

"Hi, I'm Doctor Levin. How are you feeling?"

"You need not concern yourself, sir, I am fit save for the confusion and amazement of this place."

"I'm a friend," Joseph volunteered.

"Just a few questions, Mr...what is your name?

"Daniel Rowland"

"Well Mr. Rowland, all your lab tests are fine. Where do you live?"

"My farm is in Guilford."

"Do you have any family?"

"Nay, there is only my poor wife Elizabeth who must surely be worried to distraction"

"Mr. Rowland, do you know today's date?"

"Why, it is the ninth of August."

"What year?"

"Seventeen-ninety." Doctor Levin wrote rapidly on his pad. Daniel stared at the ballpoint pen.

"What manner of pen is that?" Daniel asked.

"It's just an ordinary ballpoint..."

"Where does the ink come from?" Daniel persisted.

"It's inside the pen. Mr. Rowland, do you know the name of the president?"

"Now truly, the president is George Washington."

"I see. And where is the White House?"

"The White House?"

"Where does the president live?"

"Bless me, he lives in New York of a certainty. How does the ink get inside the pen?"

"Well, thank you Mr. Rowland." The doctor turned to leave. Joseph asked him, "Could I speak to you outside for a minute?"

In the hall, Joseph asked, "What do you think?"

"Physically he seems to be fine. Mentally...I don't really know. Maybe he's psychotic. He obviously has delusions. I'm not a psychiatrist."

"Is he dangerous? I mean do you think he would hurt someone?"

"I doubt it. I think he's harmless."

Joseph re-entered the room to find Daniel staring wide-eyed out of the window.

"My God! I dare not look again. We are so high. Those houses...buildings are so huge. The...things on the street below that move so fast. What is this place?"

Joseph gently took Daniel's arm and tried to lead him away from the window.

"It's O...it's all right, Daniel. It's all right." Daniel was stunned, but he could not turn away from the window. Joseph picked up the phone to call Linda.

"Hi, Lin? Look, I'd like to bring that guy we found home to stay with us for a while. Is that O.K.? Great. Could you pick us up? At the entrance to the Emergency Room. We'll be waiting. Bye."

"What is that?" Daniel had turned and watched Joseph talking.

"It's a phone. A telephone. I...you can talk to someone far away."

"A wonder!"

"Please put on your clothes, Daniel. You can wear those slippers. I'm taking you home with me for a visit."

While Daniel dressed, Joseph went to the nursing station and checked him out. He returned and took Daniel to stand before the elevator door. Daniel jumped back as the door opened but Joseph took his arm and they entered. As the elevator started down, Daniel crouched and yelled. The few people in the elevator turned to stare at him. The elevator made several stops on its way down. Joseph held his arm. By the time they reached street level Daniel was a little calmer. Joseph cursed himself for not having explained elevators to Daniel.

Joseph did not know what to make of Daniel. Is he a homeless person, maybe an alcoholic or a drug addict? Doctor Levin said he was some kind of psycho. But his speech, his complete unfamiliarity with everything, and those coins...Is it all an act? Anyhow, he seems harmless and very vulnerable, poor guy.

Standing outside of the Emergency Room Daniel seemed dazed.

"So many people! Pray, sir, what are these coaches? How can they move without horses?"

"They have engines that...burn fuel and...make them go."

"For the soul of me I would never have believed it. Now truly, I would to heaven I knew where I am and what is happening to me." Linda pulled up in the Toyota. Joseph opened the rear door, urged Daniel to get in.

"Daniel, this is my wife Linda."

"Hi, Daniel," Linda said with a smile as she pulled away from the entrance.

"I am very pleased to make your acquaintance, Goodwife." Daniel sat on the edge of the seat, wide-eyed, clutching the front seat with both hands.

"We are speeding very fast," he murmured. Joseph pushed him back gently.

"Relax, Daniel. Sit back and enjoy the ride,"

CHAPTER 4

"Is this truly New Haven?" Daniel asked Joseph as the car moved down York Street and turned on to Orange Street.

"Yes, it's New Haven alright. There's the Green." Daniel stared in silence.

This is not the Green I know. The buildings...so much paving...the shops...all glass...so many people...strange clothes...the women's legs all showing...My God, where am I? Linda turned on to Trumble Street and stopped at a traffic light.

"Why have we stopped, Master Pellegrini?"

"Please call me Joe." Joseph pointed to the traffic signal. "Red means stop, and green means go. They keep the traffic...the cars from running into each other."

"But the candle...it is very high...how...?"

"There's no candle. It's all electric. I'll explain later."

Linda turned on to Whitney Avenue and headed north towards Hamden. Daniel gazed in fascination at the succession of shops, businesses, and churches. He gawked at a billboard with a cigarette advertisement; an attractive model in a bathing suit holding a cigarette.

"That huge painting...?"

"It's only an ad, Daniel. That building is part of Yale University. I think it's the Forestry School."

"Now truly, I know of Yale," Daniel said, pleased at the familiar word.

Joseph continued to puzzle over Daniel's global naivete. If it was an act, he was very good. Could he be some kind of a Rip Van Winkle? No, he was just a nut like Doctor Levin said. Yet...

After thirty minutes, Linda turned on to a tree-lined street with rows of houses and parked on a driveway alongside a neat colonial with a small front lawn.

"This is home, Daniel," Linda said cheerfully. Please come in and be welcome."

"I thank you, Goodwife..." Daniel started and then broke off in confusion staring at Linda's shorts. He followed her into the house. Nick and Cathy were on the couch watching TV. Linda introduced Daniel. The youngsters stared at Daniel's clothing and the hospital slippers.

"Mr. Rowland is going to stay with us for a while," Joseph explained.

"Cool," Cathy said.

Daniel regarded the rooms. He admired the carpets, the wallpaper, the paintings, the lights and the furniture. He thought of his simple two-room farmhouse.

"For the soul of me I have never seen a house so richly furnished. It is..." A loud burst of music from the television caught his attention. "Bless me! What is that? Witchcraft? How can they...in that box?" Nick had a quizzical expression on his face. Cathy said, in her matter-of-fact way, "It's a TV. Don't they have TV where you live? Where *do* you live?" Linda interrupted.

"We're having barbecue tonight.

*

Daniel was introduced to hamburgers, hot dogs, ketchup, and potato chips, all eaten with gusto at an outdoor table in the Pellegrini back yard. He marveled at the paper plates, plastic utensils, soda, and aluminum cans. Joseph brought out three bottles of beer.

"Would you like a beer, Daniel?"

"You astonish me, Joe. May I be hanged if I ever saw ale outside of a tavern. Indeed, I will have one." The afternoon faded into a warm evening. The children went into the house to watch TV. The adults sipped their beer in silence. Joseph wondered what Daniel was thinking.

Daniel hoped that Elizabeth was able to find Nell and the wagon. Would she remember to milk Buttercup? Was she very distraught? What was she doing? When will I be able I see her?

The warm evening faded to night.

"You must be tired, Daniel," Linda said. "Joe will show you your room."

In the guestroom, Joseph explained the operation of the electric lights, the location of the bathroom and its various controls.

"Ah, a shower bath!" Daniel observed.

Joseph put a pair of pajamas on the guest bed and the morning copy of *The New Haven Register*.

"Good night, Daniel. Sleep well."

Daniel showered, put on the pajamas and got into bed. It was very firm but comfortable. He glanced around the room, noting what appeared to be small paintings or drawings of the children and other people. He was very tired. He reached for the newspaper and was surprised to see another drawing on the front page. Then he saw the date: *Friday, June 12, 1998*! It must be some mistake. That is...two hundred and...eight, no nine years from now. My now. It cannot be. It is some evil dream from which I will awake. I dare not believe...I would to Heaven I was with my Elizabeth. Daniel wept silently before falling into a restless sleep.

Downstairs, Joseph rejoined Linda in the back yard.

"What do you think?" he asked.

"Gosh, I don't know. He seems very...authentic. He's a nice guy. Maybe he worked at one of those colonial places. You know, like Mystic Seaport, and he got hit on the head in some accident and was wandering around."

"That's a good idea. But how did he get to Guilford? Anyway, I'll check it out tomorrow."

CHAPTER 5

Even before he opened his eyes, Daniel knew that the freakish events of yesterday were not just a bad dream. The unfamiliar bed, the strange style and fabric of Joe's sleeping clothes and the odor of frying bacon, all attested to the reality of what had happened to him. He remembered the date on last night's newspaper and the enormity of the time span overwhelmed him. *Two hundred and nine years!* Elizabeth and her unborn child must be d...With an effort he pushed the thought from his mind, determined not to think about it now.

He dressed and went downstairs to find Joseph and Cathy sitting at a table in the kitchen. Joseph was reading a newspaper. Cathy was eating some brown flakes in a bowl of milk and intently studying a cardboard box on the table in front of her. Linda was standing in front of some kind of a stove preparing food.

"Good morning, Daniel," she said cheerfully. "Would you like some coffee? Please sit down."

"Ah, I know of coffee, Goodwife, but I have never tasted it."

"Try some. I think you'll like it. And please call me Linda." Cathy looked up.

"Hi, Daniel. Mom, can I have a glass of milk?"

Daniel watched with interest as Linda poured some milk into a glass. He observed the shiny utensils, plates and glasses on the table. He tasted and liked the coffee. He also enjoyed the cold orange juice, the scrambled eggs, bacon and the toasted English muffin that Linda set before him.

"Would it be an indecorum for me to inquire whence comes this good food? I saw no cow. And how can you cook it without a fire? Methinks it is magic."

Cathy giggled until a sharp look from her mother stopped her mirth.

"We buy the food in a large market. Perhaps I'll take you there soon. And the cooking is all done with electricity," Linda told him.

"Joe, could you explain it to Daniel?" Joseph put down his newspaper.

"Electricity is power, it's a form of energy. It's invisible, you can't see it but it provides, heat and light, and many other things."

"How does it come into the house?"

"With wires," Joseph explained. "Wires bring the electricity from the power station to the house."

"I presume those are the ropes I saw on those many poles along the way we rode yesterday?"

"Well, yes, but they are wires, not ropes." Joseph was impressed with Daniel's powers of observation and his quick grasp of things. "The wires are made of metal" Linda showed him the range, the toaster, the refrigerator and the microwave.

"And you have your own bake oven, too." He marveled at the dishwasher.

"Bless me! How does it know when to stop washing?"

"There's a timer inside. That's electric too," Linda explained. Cathy left the kitchen to watch cartoons on TV.

"Daniel," Joseph asked casually, "How old are you?"

"I am thirty-six years of age, having been born on the tenth of March in seventeen and fifty-three."

"Can you remember anything before you woke up in the hospital?" Joseph asked him gently.

"Ah, lackaday," he replied with a deep sigh. "I was digging clams for the chowder my dear Elizabeth had a fancy to make..." Daniel described the strange black cloud and how it came ashore and overcame him. Joseph listened intently. The story was fantastic, yet it was told with such sincerity and emotion that he found himself almost believing it.

"Pray, would you take me back to Guilford, Joe? I beseech you! Mayhap I can somehow return."

"Sure, Daniel," Joseph told him sympathetically. "We'll drive over this morning. But first, let's get you some clothes and shoes." Before they left, Joseph asked Linda to phone Mystic Seaport on the off chance that Daniel had been working there.

*

Joseph took Daniel to a small department store in Hamden. Daniel was amazed at the variety and quantity of clothing on the racks and shelves. Joseph found two pair of slacks for Daniel, several sport shirts, some underwear and socks, and a pair of loafers. Daniel didn't know any of his sizes so measurements had to be taken. Joseph paid for the purchases with a credit card and tried to explain to Daniel why it was not necessary to pay for the clothes with money.

The next stop was the Hamden police station.

"This man has amnesia," Joseph explained to the desk sergeant, "and we're trying to find out who he is. He can't remember anything except his name. Can you help?" The sergeant was very sympathetic.

"No problem," he said. "We can take a shot of him and send his prints to the FBI. If he's ever been in the Armed Forces or worked for the government, or has a criminal record, they'll be able to identify him. Hey, Nancy," he called out. "Come up here."

Daniel became nervous at the talk of shooting him, and when an uniformed policewoman appeared wearing a pistol on her belt, he considered running out of the station. She beckoned for Daniel and Joseph to follow her and she led them to a room where she took Daniel's fingerprints. She gave Daniel a paper towel to wipe the ink from his fingers. In another room she took several photos of him. As they left the police station, Joseph explained fingerprinting to Daniel.

"Every print is different," Joseph told him. "No two people are alike. Criminals often leave their prints at the crime scene. The police can detect the prints and if they capture the criminal they can compare his prints to the ones they found at the crime scene." Joseph also explained photography to Daniel, who now understood the many "drawings" and "paintings" he had seen.

"We'll go to Guilford now," Joseph told him.

*

Daniel's face brightened as they passed the sign marking the exit to Leete's Island on their way to Guilford.

"Leete's Island!" he exclaimed. "I know it well."

"What can you tell me about it?" Joseph asked.

"I was wont to dig for clams there many a day. It is only an island when the tide is in. Much of the land belongs to old Jordan Leete but he has given parcels to his kinsmen Palatiah, Solomon, and Daniel, Junior, all of them Leetes. Solomon's place is near the West Road. Ambrose Leete has a house and barn up from Turkey Point on the west pasture and Thomas Leete has a house near the East Road. Captain Noah Fowler has a lot there, near to Crooper Hill, but no house. And two years ago Thomas Hart and Simeon Leete built houses there. Simeon's house is near the West Road and the Hart House is near to the East Road."

Joseph was astonished by all the detail. Was Daniel making this stuff up? Had he researched Leete's Island somewhere? But why?

They continued along I-95 to the Guilford exit. The road became Church Street and led to the Green. Daniel became agitated as they passed the Congregational Church at the north end of the Green.

"The church...it is different. Our Puritan Church stood there with the steeple clock that Ebenezer Parmelee, our Town Clerk, made with his own hands and gave to the church. The school...is gone...that brick building there." Joseph drove slowly around the Green. Daniel stared intently, shaking his head.

"Where was...is your farm, Daniel?"

"To the east at Hammonasset, near the Stage Road."

Joseph continued east along Route 1, the Boston Post Road. After a several miles the road crossed railroad tracks. Daniel stared at them briefly but didn't ask for an explanation. They passed through the tiny town of Madison, with an ancient church on the green. A sign read "First Congregation Church, 1707." Daniel grew excited.

"The church...it still stands. I...we went there. And there stands the house of Deacon John Graves," he said as they passed a nearby structure. They reached the connecting road that led back to I-95. Off to the right stretched the gravelly beaches of Hammonasset State Park and the blue waters of Long Island Sound.

"Which way now, Daniel?"

"Go on, Joe" Less than a hundred yards ahead they reached an unpaved road marked "Mill Road." Daniel signaled for Joseph to turn left. He drove slowly, passing a pond on the right.

"My farm...it was beyond the river. Joseph drove slowly on. A half-mile further, on the left, was a large graveyard. The sign read "Hammonasset Cemetery, 1658."

"Our burying ground," Daniel said quietly. "May we enter?"

The gate was locked forcing them to climb over the low stone wall. Most of the markers were recent but in the southeast corner of the cemetery they found a section with older gravestones. They walked to the old section, pausing to read the names on the markers. Many were no longer readable but Daniel was able to discern some names and dates.

"Jedediah Coe, 1803. He was my neighbor. Captain Phineas Meigs, 1782. We knew him. A fine man. Reuben Hill, 1835. His wife Hannah, 1833. Deacon Thomas Stone, 1797. They were our friends and neighbors," intoned Daniel.

A small marker of reddish colored stone stood by itself at the end of the row of graves. Daniel walked to it, paused to read, and then sank to his knees with a choked cry.

"Oh my God..."

Joseph walked to the stone.

Elizabeth Rowland
Wife of Daniel
d. 1828 AE 62

Daniel was weeping and sobbing.

"Oh Elizabeth. Oh my dear one," he cried. "I would to heaven I were with you. I am so wretched." Joseph knelt near Daniel and put his arm around his shoulders to comfort him.

He is mourning for a woman who died a hundred and seventy years ago, he thought. But to Daniel it was as if she had died yesterday. He led Daniel back to the car. They continued east on Route 1, and crossed the Hammonasset River into Clinton. Daniel wept silently.

"Pray turn here, Joe."

Joseph turned left on Highland Drive, a short street that ended after one block. Ahead was a large meadow.

"Our farm...it was hither. Yon stood our house, the barn, Abigail's grave..." The only evidence of human activity was a sign that read "Police Range" and pointed to the meadow. As they looked, a train passed somewhere in the distance beyond the meadow.

"Please, Joe, could you bring me back to where you found me?" Joseph. nodded. They drove back to Guilford, parked at the end of Dunk Rock Road and walked down the trail toward the beach.

"Here's where we found you, Daniel."

"Pray, wait here for me, Joe."

Daniel walked to the beach. The day was overcast and the tide was out. He looked around for something, anything, but the sand had no footprints except his own. He walked to the water's edge and stared out to sea. The horizon was indistinct.

"Please," he called. "I beseech you!" He stretched his arms out and shouted, "Come back! Take me back." He fell to his knees, weeping, pleading, and entreating. "I beg you," he sobbed to the sky. "Take me home."

CHAPTER 6

For the next several weeks Daniel was inconsolable. At times he could be heard weeping in his room. Joseph and Linda tried unsuccessfully to cheer him up but it was Cathy who finally broke through his grief.

It was a warm Sunday afternoon. Joseph and Linda had gone shopping. Nick was at a friend's house, and Cathy was playing in the back yard. Suddenly she began to scream. She had unearthed a nest of yellow jackets and they swarmed around and stung her repeatedly.

"Daniel," she screamed. Daniel raced down from his room to the yard. He scooped the girl up in his arms, swatting the stinging bees with his hands. When the insects were all dead or gone, he mixed some soil with water to make a paste and applied it to the child's stings. In a few minutes the pain began to subside and Cathy stopped crying.

"Thanks, Daniel," she said. She went inside to the bathroom and emerged laughing.

"I'm all covered with mud," she told Daniel. "How did you know to do that?"

"Pshaw! Everyone knows to put mud upon a bee sting."

"When can I wash it off?"

"Whenever you fancy. You need not keep it."

"I'm going to leave it on," she said brightly. "I want to scare Mom."

"Well, I will say you look for all the world like a Red Indian."

"Did you know any Indians?"

"Even so. The Uncas were friendly and traded with us but the Pequots were our enemies and raided us in the old days."

"I'm sorry about your wife, Daniel," Cathy said quietly.

Daniel nodded gravely, then smiled at her.

*

"Do you believe that Daniel is really from back there...back then?" Cathy asked her brother.

"No, like how could he get here? He'd be over a hundred years old. I mean no one lives that long. He looks younger than Dad."

"But couldn't he like, fall asleep, like that guy in the story with the dog and the gun?" his sister persisted.

"You mean Rip van Winkle. That's just a made up story. Besides, *he* got old."

"I don't care. I like him."

Nick shrugged and went off to meet with some friends.

*

Linda was very appreciative of Daniel's assistance to Cathy. She liked him and although she was suspicious of his authenticity she found his quaint speech interesting and charming. As time went on, she began to regard him with a mixture of sympathy and affection. What impressed her most about Daniel was his artless candor. He was reserved but not devious. He seldom volunteered an opinion but if he was questioned he gave all he had. Almost everything Daniel encountered was novel to him and Linda began to take pleasure in introducing him to each new thing, giving him reasons and explanations.

"He's so simple and intelligent," she confided to Joseph. "I feel he's like a big kid eager to learn about everything."

She began to consider that perhaps Daniel was indeed who he claimed to be, although the manner of his getting here remained a mystery. She treated him as genuine. Joseph felt compelled to continue his investigation.

*

The police sergeant phoned to report that Daniel's fingerprint search had come up negative. The FBI had no record of Daniel. Further checks with the Social Security Administration, the FAA, and the Connecticut Department of Motor Vehicles revealed nothing.

Joseph recalled the two coins he found in Daniel's clothing at the hospital and he decided to check their authenticity. He located a numismatist in Milford and brought the coins. Mr. Edward Dorian, an expert in old coins, examined them carefully.

"May I ask where you got these?" he asked. "There are very few around and these are in very fine condition." Joseph avoided the question.

"Are they authentic?" he persisted.

"Indeed they are." The numismatist explained that in colonial times coins were in very short supply and that a mint had been established in New Haven to produce them.

"Are they valuable?" Joseph asked. Mr. Dorian consulted a manual.

"These are worth between one thousand and fifteen hundred dollars...each. Are you interested in selling them?"

"Not at this time." Joseph thanked him and left, more confused than ever.

*

Of the myriad devices that Daniel encountered each day, television intrigued him the most. He watched TV for hours, intrigued by the music and dancing and fascinated by the soap operas. He was embarrassed by the sex and love scenes and appalled by the violence. He enjoyed the sports, wondered at the news and talk shows, and felt pressured and confused by the commercials. He was incredulous at the sight of trains, airplanes, helicopters, ships, submarines, space ships and men walking on the moon. He also saw horses.

"How can those guns fire so many times without reloading? Can men truly fly in those...coaches? Do ships indeed move under the sea? Pray Joe, what is space? What has become of horses?"

Joseph attempted to answer those and the many other questions Daniel put to him. He assured Daniel of the truth of modern methods of transportation. He took Daniel to the Tweed-New Haven Airport so that he could actually see the small airplanes landing and taking off. He drove him to Groton and New London to view the ships and submarines. Joseph also found a stable nearby in Hamden that kept horses.

Daniel enjoyed the visit to the Hamden Riding Stable more than anything else. He inhaled the familiar stable smells of urine and manure as if they were rare perfumes, petted the horses and watched them being led in and out of their stalls. He inspected and admired the saddles and bridles and he conversed with the stable hands. They found his speech somewhat strange but they assumed he was a foreigner.

"Come around whenever you like," one of them told Daniel as he and Joseph were leaving.

"They remind me of my Nell," he explained to Joseph.

*

"This is of course hypothetical," Joseph asked his friend, Professor Alex Gifford, "but how could one distinguish a man of colonial times from a man of the present era?" They were having lunch in the Quinnipiac cafeteria.

"That's an interesting question, Joe. Let me think for a moment." Dr. Gifford, a microbiologist in the Health Sciences Department, took a mouthful of his sandwich. "Well," he continued, "most men of our era received the standard pediatric immunizations—you know, diphtheria, tetanus, whooping cough, polio—when we were kids, and may still have circulating antibodies to those. A colonial man wouldn't be expected to have those antibodies unless he actually had those diseases."

"Anything else?" Joe asked. "How about DNA?"

"I don't see how DNA would help, but I thought of two other things. Most men today still have the scar of smallpox vaccination on their arm or leg. You wouldn't find this on a colonial man because vaccination wasn't in widespread use then. Oh yes, and most men today have had some dental work; fillings, crowns, and such that weren't available in colonial days."

"Thanks, Alex, that's very helpful. Where could I get such tests done?" Alex looked at him curiously.

"I can draw the blood specimen and get the tests done in a clinical laboratory. There'll be a charge."

"That's O.K., Alex. I'll bring you the blood."

*

Nick passed his driving test and Joseph let him have limited use of the family Toyota during the day. Nick now volunteered to run any errands that would give him the opportunity to drive. He took Daniel for rides to the stable and to some small nearby farms. Daniel often got into conversations with some of the farmers and learned about chemical fertilizer, tractors, milking machines, crop rotation, irrigation and insecticides. Nick listened to these discussions with curiosity.

"Mark you," Daniel told Nick as they drove home one afternoon, "I used fish and seaweed to enrich the soil. And I planted my crops in a different field each year. As for the beetles and crows, I just planted extra. We used to say 'One for the blackbird, one for the crow, one for the cutworm and one to grow'."

Nick became interested in what Daniel told him about shearing sheep, carding, spinning and weaving, hunting, trapping, separating grain from chaff, milling, and a hundred other things. Nick was very impressed. He told some of his friends about Daniel. One of those boys told his father, who worked as a printer for the *New Haven Register*.

Daniel became a frequent visitor at the stable whenever Nick would drive him there. The stable hands soon learned that Daniel knew about horses and had a way with them. They were more than happy to have him help clean the stalls, feed and water the animals, and rub them down after they were ridden.

*

"You know, Daniel, you really should have a check-up," Joseph told him one afternoon.

"Check-up?"

"A medical and dental examination."

"Forsooth, Joe, I do not discover that I am ill and I am not disposed to..."

"Trust me, Daniel. It is just to make sure that there are no ill effects from that black cloud."

Daniel eventually agreed and Joseph lost no time in contacting his physician.

"I want you to examine him for evidence of a vaccination scar."

"That's all?"

"That and draw several tubes of blood for antibody studies." After the examination the doctor told Joseph, "I couldn't find any vaccination scar. I drew the blood. You can pick it up at my office. What's this all about?"

"If I told you, you wouldn't believe it."

Joseph brought the tubes of blood to Alex. He also called his dentist and made an appointment for Daniel.

"How are his teeth?" Joseph inquired afterward.

"Pretty good, a few small cavities"

"Has he seen a dentist before this?"

"If he has, nothing was done. There's no evidence of any previous dental work. Has he been away somewhere?"

"Sort of," Joseph told him before hanging up.

Two weeks later Joseph met Alex for lunch.

"I have your report," Alex told him.

"Well?"

"Completely negative. He has no antibodies to diphtheria, polio, whooping cough or tetanus. I guess they missed giving him the shots."

Joseph was becoming a believer in spite of himself.

CHAPTER 7

The summer was coming to an end. Joseph returned to the Quinnipiac campus, Linda commenced teaching at the high school, and Nick and Cathy went back to their schools. Daniel often found himself at loose ends, waiting for the family to come home at the end of the day. On some days, Joseph dropped Daniel off at the stable where he spent the hours happily working with the horses. Other days he would remain at home watching the TV. He longed for something useful to do and he drummed his fingers hour after hour. He was accustomed to arising early and working a long, hard day. The many idle hours made him uneasy.

Daniel was now on familiar terms with a toothbrush, toothpaste, safety razors, shaving cream in a can and indoor plumbing. He was amused at Linda's vacuum cleaner and the various products she used to clean and maintain the house. Nick taught him how to start the lawn mower, and Daniel kept the grass cut. On several occasions, he accompanied Linda to the supermarket. She had to assure him that the many women using lipstick were not harlots.

"Now truly, there are vittles here enow to feed a village for a year," Daniel marveled. "May I be hanged if I have ever seen so much food. Whence comes it all?" Linda smiled.

"It's brought in by trucks and railroad from farms and dairies all over the country. Some of the trucks are refrigerated." Daniel stopped to gaze at the live lobsters in a tank.

"I am astonished. I presume that this market is only for the rich…"

"No," Linda told him. "It's for everybody."

On the checkout line, Daniel stared in amazement at the automatic tallying of the groceries and the rapid exchange of bills and coins.

"Upon my word," he said quietly. "It is all so quick. And so easy!"

*

"Joe," Daniel said one evening, "alas, I have no money. I am wont to seek some work. Methought some farm nearby...?"

"You will need a Social Security card," Joseph told him. "I'll help you get one. In the meantime, do you remember these?" He produced the two copper coins.

"Ah, two pence. They would buy little here."

"They are worth a lot of money now. Shall I sell them for you?"

Daniel nodded assent.

*

"I'd like to sell these now," Joseph told the numismatist.

"I can offer you twenty-five hundred dollars for the two," Mr. Dorian said. Joseph gave the money to Daniel that evening.

"Bless me!" Daniel exclaimed. "More than two thousand dollars for tuppence. I am truly a rich man. This is enough money to buy a large farm." Joseph and Linda laughed.

"Take care of it, Daniel," Linda told him. "It won't last forever."

*

At the Social Security Office in New Haven, Daniel completed the application with Joseph's assistance and brought it to the clerk.

"I can't accept this," the clerk said. "You put down 1753 as your birth date. You must mean 1953. Go change it."

"That is my true birth year," Daniel told him.

"Not in this office it ain't, mister. Next!" Daniel turned away in confusion and the next person on line took his place. Joseph shrugged.

"We'll think of something."

*

"You have much work, Friend Harmon. This is indeed a large farm." Daniel was talking to Harmon Platt, a farmer he visited several times.

"Naa, it's only a hundred and sixty acres. But I guess I could use some help. You interested?"

"Indeed, I am, but I am unable to obtain the Social Security card and..." Harmon laughed.

"I don't care a hoot about that. You come around and see me and we'll work something out."

*

Joseph was determined to inform Daniel of the many things that had happened during the last two hundred years. This was no easy task even for a history professor. He suggested that Daniel might like to attend some of his history classes. Daniel was amazed at the diversity of the students on the campus and he questioned Joseph about some of them.

"The black ones are probably the descendants of slaves that were brought here in your time," Joseph explained. "The students with the little skullcaps are Jews; the ones with turbans are Hindus or Moslems from India or Pakistan and the oriental ones are probably from China or Japan."

"The killers of our Lord and heathens at a Christian university?" Daniel inquired. "Are not the Jews an accursed race condemned to wander the earth...?"

"Actually it was German mercenaries in the Roman Army who crucified Jesus," Joseph told him. "The Jews have contributed much to our civilization. They have their own country called Israel. And we now recognize other religions as meaningful forms of belief. We don't call them heathens anymore. Oh, and by the way, this is a private, secular university."

"Ah," Daniel said, "German mercenaries. The British used Hessians against us in the war. They are cruel fighters." He paused for a moment. "To which church do *you* belong, Joe? I have noticed that you and Linda do not attend Sunday services."

"We're Roman Catholic. Linda was Episcopalian but she converted. Actually neither of us is very religious."

"A papist!" Daniel exclaimed. "Well, no man could want a finer friend than you, Joe. But do you truly worship statues and such?"

"No," Joseph told him patiently with a smile. "I'm late for a class. Why don't you come along?"

The class was History 561, Studies in New England History.

"I have a surprise for you today," Joseph announced to the students. "Meet Mister Daniel Rowland, born in Guilford 1n 1753. He can tell us much about life in colonial Connecticut". The class laughed.

"You must mean *19*53, Professor Pellegrini," one of the students said.

"No, I meant 1753," Joseph said with a smile.

"That would make him more than two hundred years old," the student said in confusion. A few students laughed nervously.

"Correct." There was stunned silence in the class. Another student asked "Is this some kind of a joke...a test or something?"

"It's no joke," Joseph told them seriously.

"But how...?"

"I don't know. He doesn't know. There's no explanation. He's just here." The class was silent. Daniel remained standing awkwardly in front of the class. One of the students brought him a chair.

"Daniel," Joseph asked, "would you mind telling the class about the...you know...about the cloud and everything that happened to you?" Daniel nodded and related the events of that day. The students listened with rapt attention.

"and that was the last I knew until I awakened in the New Haven...Hospital."

"We found him lying on the beach in Guilford." Joseph added.

"Who was the governor of Connecticut then?" one of the students challenged.

"Of a certainty it was Samuel Huntington, the lawyer from Norwich," Daniel answered.

"Was he a Democrat or a Republican?" another asked.

"I do not understand those words."

"What was his party?" Joseph explained.

"Ah, he was a Federalist." The class was briefly quiet. Then another student asked, "How was Guilford founded?" Daniel smiled.

"The six founders were Puritan gentlemen from Surrey and Kent in England. There was Henry Whitfield, the leader, Robert Kitchell, William Leete, William Chittenden, John Bishop and John Coffinge. They landed in New Haven and bought the land from the Indians. The Indians called it Menunkatuk. That was back in 1649. We learned that in school."

"Who was the governor before Huntington?"

"It was Mathew Griswold, from Lyme. He was a Federalist too and he had a house in Guilford near to East Creek." The questions continued, increasing in complexity.

"Do you remember any Guilford officials?"

"Of a certainty," Daniel replied. "Thomas Burgis is...was the magistrate, Ebenezer Parmalee was the Town Clerk, Nathaniel Ruggles was the doctor..."

"How about the State Supreme Court. Who were the judges?" another student interrupted.

"Pray permit me to think. My head is addled. Yes. Eliphalet Dyer was the chief judge, and there was Andrew Adams and Jesse Root, and two others I disremember." The questions continued. The students were trying to test Daniel, to catch him and prove he was a fraud. Joseph was astounded at the details recounted by Daniel. He had questions too but the clock indicated that the class was over and the students rose to leave. One of the students enthusiastically congratulated Joseph.

"Great routine, Professor! How much do you have to pay him?"

"That was the most interesting and exciting account I ever heard, Mr. Rowland."

Daniel turned to see a pretty, petite, tan-skinned young woman with oriental features, smiling at him.

"Hi," she said, extending her hand. "I'm Betsy Abrahams. I just wanted to tell you that I don't care how you got here. I'm very glad you're here." Daniel shook her hand clumsily. He was embarrassed by her directness and he didn't know what to say. He just smiled at her. She joined Daniel and Joseph as they walked back to Joseph's office.

"Betsy is very interested in early Connecticut history," Joseph told Daniel. "I'm sure she has many questions for you." Daniel smiled at her and nodded.

"Would you like to join us for lunch?" Joseph asked her.

"I have another class now," she said. "Bye, Professor. I hope to see you again soon, Mr. Rowland."

CHAPTER 8

The two were inmates at the Statesville Correction Center in Joliet, Illinois. Tony, from Chicago, was serving five to ten years for armed robbery. Carlos, who shared his cell, was from Detroit and was serving ten to twenty years for a murder he committed during a holdup of a Springfield gas station. He had been in Joliet for eight years. This was not their first incarceration; Tony had a long record of felony convictions going back to his teens. He worked in the prison library and read extensively. He had served four years of his present sentence.

Carlos was assigned to work in the prison laundry. He made up in cunning what he lacked in intelligence. A product of the ghetto, he dreamed of wealth. More specifically, he considered committing crimes that would make him rich. Together, Tony and Carlos evaluated burglary, robbery, kidnapping for ransom, arson, various types of fraud, and other felonies for their potential for gain and the risk of apprehension.

"It's banks, man," Tony concluded. "That's where the real bread is at."

"But they got guards," Carlos told him.

"Naa, not any more. Not the little ones. I bin reading. And they don't carry no heat," Tony told him.

"It's a Federal rap," Carlos added.

"So what. Look, you get in fast, show 'em a piece and a note. You grab a sack of Benjamins, everybody's panicked and you beat it before they know what the hell happened. By the time the cops arrive, you're long gone."

"I don't know, man," Carlos wavered.

"And you pull one, two good jobs and you can retire."

They had many such discussions. Tony was certain that bank robbery was the most rewarding crime. Gradually, Carlos was convinced and they became more and more enthusiastic about the idea. Then they began to make plans.

*

Joseph wondered about how to bring Daniel up to date.

How should I present the events of the last two hundred years? Should I organize them by topic, such as wars, great inventions and discoveries, geopolitical changes and so forth? Or should I relate these events chronologically, as they happened? And should I limit them to the United States or should I include the whole world? He decided to get a student's viewpoint and he asked Betsy Abrahams what she thought about it. Betsy was very flattered by being asked for her opinion.

"I think that you should tell him about all the important things that happened, as they happened," she told him. "and especially the things that would or could affect him as an American."

Joseph thought that system sounded reasonable and as good as any other. Betsy asked if she could attend these sessions.

"Oh, please, please, Professor," she enthused. "He's such an interesting man and he must have so many fascinating things to tell *us* about." Joseph smiled and nodded his assent.

"O.K., I'll let you know when."

*

A few weeks later, Daniel, Joseph and Betsy gathered in the Pellegrini living room. Daniel and Betsy were seated on a couch facing Joseph. A large map of the United States was placed on a low coffee table between them.

"Let's see," Joseph asked Daniel, "you...left in 1790?" Daniel nodded.

"Well in 1792, the French people decided that they had enough of the way their king, that was Louis the sixteenth, handled the country's money. They had a huge debt as a result of their participation in *our* revolution, so they staged their own revolution. They abolished the monarchy, executed the king and started a reign of terror that led to the guillotining of thousands of people, mostly aristocrats."

"What is guillotine?" Daniel asked.

"It's a device with a big knife that cuts off people's heads."

"What happened?" Daniel asked.

"The French established a republic that lasted seven years when Napoleon Bonaparte, one of their generals, overthrew the established government and ruled France as Emperor.

"So their revolution was a failure," Daniel commented.

"Not completely. France was unified, and the effects of their revolution were felt throughout Europe. Ancient social structures, like feudalism, were torn down and the precedents of democratic institutions, like elections and constitutions, were established." Joseph called attention to the map on the table.

"In 1803, our country purchased this huge block of land from France. It was called Louisiana. It was right in the center of North America. The area extended from the Mississippi River to the Rocky Mountains, and from the Gulf of Mexico to what is now Canada. The land now includes the states of Louisiana, Arkansas, Missouri, Minnesota, North and South Dakota, Nebraska, Oklahoma, Kansas, Montana, Wyoming, Colorado and part of Florida." Joseph showed Daniel the area on the map.

"I count thirteen states," Daniel said excitedly. "That would be in addition to our original thirteen. Pray, how many states are there now?"

"Fifty."

"Upon my word!" Daniel gasped. "So many."

"There's more to come," Joseph told him. "In 1812, we went to war with England again."

"Oho! The villains. I presume they wanted to become the masters of their former colonies."

"No, that wasn't it. England had lost the American market and was suffering financially. The border between the United States and Canada around the Great Lakes was contested, and the Royal Navy was stopping American vessels on the high seas and impressing our merchant seamen into their crews. Also, there was a group in Congress that wanted the United States to seize Canada. President James Madison declared war. We tried to invade Canada, but we were repulsed. Our navy was badly defeated on the Atlantic but we won a victory on Lake Erie. Two years later, British forces seized and burned Washington." Daniel was aghast.

"You astonish me. They burned General Washington?"

"No, the city of Washington."

"Where, I pray, is Washington? I do not discover the location of that city."

"Washington is our national capital. It is on the banks of the Potomac River, near Maryland and Virginia. It settled the rivalry between Northern and Southern states for the location of the national capital. George Washington selected the exact spot. He was a surveyor, you know. The White House, where the president resides, was started in 1792. Thomas Jefferson was the first president to be inaugurated in the new capital."

"I dare not ask who won the war?"

"Andrew Jackson defeated the Redcoats at the Battle of New Orleans, and the war was over, but no one really won."

"I think that's the way of all wars," Betsy added. "No one really wins." Joseph continued.

"The first steamship crossed the Atlantic from Savannah, Georgia to Liverpool in 1819. The trip took twenty-nine days."

"The Mayflower took two months to cross the sea," Daniel said.

"The first railroad to be pulled by a steam locomotive was in Massachusetts in 1825 and ten years later, the telegraph was invented; the first system for directly communicating over long distances by wire."

"Astonishing!" Joseph smiled.

"It's obsolete now, Daniel. Anyway, the Union grew larger again when we annexed Texas. That led to the Mexican War from which we gained Texas, New Mexico and California. Our country now stretched across the continent, from the Atlantic to the Pacific. A few years later, we purchased more land, what is now the state of Arizona, from Mexico. Gold was discovered in California, and the Congress offered one hundred and sixty acres of land, at $1.25 an acre, to anyone who would live on the land for five years."

"A hundred and sixty acres for, let me see, that comes to two hundred dollars. That is enough land for eight farms, and for only two hundred dollars."

"Yes, that offer and the rush to find gold caused thousands of settlers to move to the West."

Betsy half-stifled a yawn. Daniel stretched.

"I guess that's enough for one evening," Joseph announced.

*

Betsy and Daniel saw each other often since their first meeting in Joseph's class. She soon overcame his shyness and they became friends. Betsy was little more than five feet tall, with a trim, athletic figure, usually encased in tight-fitting jeans. She had jet-black hair, worn in a ponytail, a *café au lait* complexion and slightly slanted eyes that gave her an elfin appearance. She played cello in the college orchestra. She was very outspoken but she managed to put Daniel at ease.

"Jamaica is a melting pot." she explained to Daniel. "My mother is Chinese and my father is Jamaican. I think one of his parents was Jewish." Daniel smiled at her. Although she was twenty, she still had girlish ways and Daniel had begun to think of her as a younger sister.

"What kinds of games did you play when you were a child?" she asked him one afternoon, as they strolled on one of the campus walks.

"Oh, we played *Ring Around a Rosie* and *Oats, Peas, Beans and Barley*.

"How does that one go?"

Daniel stopped walking, folded his arms across his chest and sang:

Oats, peas, beans and barley grow.
Oats, peas, beans and barley grow.
Can you or I or anyone know,
How oats, peas, beans and barley grow? Daniel made the gesture of sowing seeds.

First the farmer sows his seed,
Then he stands and takes his ease.
He stamps his foot and claps his hand," Daniel stamped his foot and clapped his hands.

"*Then turns around and views the land."*

Daniel walked in a small circle and then shaded his eyes with his hand. Betsy was delighted.

"That's great!" she cried. "What other songs did you sing?" Daniel chuckled.

"There was *Yankee Doodle, The Golden Vanity, Johnny Has Gone for a Soldier.* There were hymns, *We Gather Together* and *Praise God from Whom All Blessings Flow*. The British played *The World Turned Upside Down* and *The Girl I Left Behind Me*."

Betsy was absolutely certain that Daniel was authentic. She couldn't explain how he came to be here but she believed everything he told her. She was also becoming very fond of him.

*

Joseph took copious and detailed notes of everything that Daniel told him about his life in Guilford. He spent several days in the Historical Room of the Guilford Free Library researching the information that Daniel provided. It was accurate. Joseph was very troubled. Daniel claimed to be from 1790. He was never vaccinated or immunized. He had no dental work. He carried coins of the era. His clothes were hand sewn, no labels. His speech was archaic. There was no record of him in Washington; as far as the government was concerned, Daniel didn't exist. Joseph had no rational way of dealing with the appearance of a living 18th century man in the 20th century.

CHAPTER 9

The phone rang one evening after dinner. Joseph picked it up.

"Professor Pellegrini?"

"Yes."

"Professor, my name is Bob Hunt. I'm a reporter for *The New Haven Register*. Someone told me that you have a guest who claims to be two hundred years old. Is that true?"

"Well..." Joseph stammered.

"Could I come over and discuss this with you?"

Joseph tried to prepare Daniel for the reporter's visit. "Somehow they found out about you," he told Daniel. "He'll just want to ask questions."

"I am not disposed to tell a long tale," Daniel said. "I know little of what happened."

"Just tell him the truth as best you can."

"Fear not, Joe. I shall relate whatever I am able.

Thirty minutes later, Joseph admitted the reporter, a man in his early forties.

"Professor Pellegrini? Hi, I'm Bob Hunt from the *Register*." Joseph brought him into the living room and introduced him to Daniel.

"This is Mr. Daniel Rowland."

"Hello, Mr. Rowland," the reporter said, shaking Daniel's hand. "I'm Bob Hunt from the *New Haven Register*."

"I am pleased to make your acquaintance, sir," Daniel responded somewhat nervously. They all sat down. The reporter took out a pad and pencil.

"You don't mind if I take some notes?" he asked. "Tell me something about yourself, Mr. Rowland," the reporter began. "Where were you born?"

"I was born in Guilford, Connecticut."

"And when was that?"

"Sir?"

"What was the date of your birth?"

"Ah, I was born on the tenth of March, seventeen and fifty-three."

"And how old are you?"

"My age is thirty-six years."

"Mr. Rowland, do you know what year this is?"

"Indeed, sir, it is 1998."

"Well, Mr. Rowland, that would seem to make you two hundred and forty-five years old. I must say you don't look much older than thirty-six. How do you account for that?" Daniel shrugged.

"Can you tell me how...and when, you came to be here?"

Daniel related his encounter with the dark cloud. Joseph went on to tell of finding Daniel on the beach, staying with him in the hospital and bringing him home. He described Daniel's clothing, the coins, lack of any previous dental work, no evidence of vaccinations, and his complete familiarity with the people and events of his time.

"That's extremely interesting," the reporter said. "How can you explain it?"

"I can't explain it," Joseph told him.

"What do you think of our time, Mr. Rowland?"

"Ah forsooth sir, it is a wonderment. So many people. Everything moves very fast. Your life is easy. You have so many comforts, and yet..."

"And yet?" the reporter asked.

"I would fain return...to my time," Daniel said quietly.

"What is your field, Professor?" the reporter asked, after furiously writing in his notepad.

"History," Joseph told him.

"Any special period?"

"The American colonial period."

"That's very interesting too. Quite a coincidence, wouldn't you say? Well, thank you both and good-night."

The story appeared in the newspaper two days later:

QUINNIPIAC PROFESSOR HOSTS VISITOR FROM 1700'S

By Tom Hunt

HAMDEN, CT.-Joseph Pellegrini, 45, a history professor at Quinnipiac College, has been entertaining Daniel Rowland, who claims to have come from colonial Guilford, and who insists that he was born in 1753. Mr. Rowland stated that he lived on his farm in Guilford during the American Revolution and that he arrived in our era by travelling on a black cloud that set him down on the beach in Guilford. He did not disclose the purpose of his visit. Professor Pellegrini stated that he has verified his visitor's origin, and that he accepts Mr. Rowland's claims as valid.

*

The phone rang in Joseph's office the next morning.

"Ah Joseph, this is Dean Stone. How are you?"

"I'm fine, thanks, Dean Stone." Joseph's stomach tightened. He knew what was coming.

"Ah Joseph, this story in the *Register*. How did that happen?"

"It's difficult to explain."

"Could you come over to my office, whenever it's convenient, and we could discuss it?"

"I'll be right over, Dean Stone." A few minutes later, Joseph was seated in the Dean's office.

"You must realize, Joseph," the dean said, "that this kind of story doesn't enhance the college's reputation. It makes you...all of us, appear foolish. And it's all nonsense."

"I'm afraid not," Joseph said. "It's true."

"What? How could that be? You know that's not possible."

"I can't explain it, Dean Stone, but I must tell you that I believe it."

"Joseph," the dean said patiently, "you're a historian. This is the sort of thing you probably wish would happen, so you could learn a lot about that era, but time travel is science fiction. It doesn't exist. The man is a fraud or else he's psychotic."

"Would you at least be willing to meet him?" Joseph pleaded. "Then you could judge for yourself."

"I...well, all right. Have him here tomorrow."

After Joseph left, the dean picked up the phone and called his secretary.

"I want to speak to Doctor Irwin Rosenbach. He's in the Psychiatry Department at the Yale School of Medicine."

*

The following morning, Joseph and Daniel were shown into the dean's office to find the dean and another man waiting for them.

"Professor Pellegrini, this is Doctor Rosenbach. He's a psychiatrist. And this, I presume, is Mr. Rowland?" There were awkward handshakes.

"Joseph," the dean began, "I asked Doctor Rosenbach to be here so that he could meet Mr. Rowland and perhaps ask him some questions. Would that be O.K.?" Joseph grimly forced a smile and turned to Daniel.

"Would you mind talking to him?"

"Nay," Daniel said agreeably. "I would be pleased to talk with the good doctor as long as he wishes."

"Good," the dean said, obviously relieved. "They can use this room." He led Daniel and the psychiatrist to an adjoining conference room and returned to join Joseph.

"I really feel that this will...uh, clarify things," he said apologetically. "And the whole business will be forgotten in a few days."

They sat in a strained silence for over an hour, punctuated be occasional phone calls that the dean answered. After what seemed like an interminable period, the door opened and Daniel and the psychiatrist entered. Both were smiling.

"Will *you* want to talk to Daniel?" Joseph asked the dean. Dean Stone turned to Daniel. "What is your occupation, Mr. Rowland?"

"I am a farmer."

"Have you had any education?"

"Indeed sir, precious little. I went to school for two months each winter for four years. I learned to write and to read and to cipher."

"What things do...did you read?"

"Why sir, when I wasn't working of a Sunday, I read our bible. And when I could visit our library, I read the almanac and the newspaper from New Haven."

"Well, thank you for coming in, Mr. Rowland. It was a pleasure meeting you." The dean rose and extended his hand.

After Joseph and Daniel left his office, the dean questioned the psychiatrist.

"Well, Irwin, what do you think?"

"He scored thirty on the Mini-Mental Status, which is completely normal, and..."

"Never mind the psychiatric double-talk," the dean interrupted. "Is he a nut case?"

"He obviously has a delusional disorder," the psychiatrist told him. "This may be a manifestation of some underlying psychosis, but more extensive evaluation would be necessary to make that determination. I'd want an MRI to rule out head trauma and an EEG for epileptoid states. Maybe he's a case of multiple personality. Otherwise, he seems quite normal. A very pleasant man. Interesting."

The Associated Press picked up the story and articles appeared in newspapers throughout the country. Some of the stories suggested that Joseph and Daniel were perpetrating a hoax for some commercial purpose. The telephone in Joseph's house rang incessantly with requests from radio and television stations for interviews with Daniel. Joseph refused them all. Several of the tabloids wanted to do a story about Daniel and one suggested that he was a visitor from another universe. The tension grew day after day. Nick and Cathy complained to their parents that their schoolmates were teasing them. A reporter hounded Linda at her school. The dean called again.

"Joseph, I think you should make a statement to the media, denying that you believe Rowland's story. Perhaps it would be wise if he were institutionalized for a while to get some treatment."

"I can't do that, Dean Stone. I *do* believe him."

*

Karen Sanders was relaxing on Dwight's couch, sipping a Coke and telling him about one of her professors.

"He's really quite good," she went on, "and he has the most terrific imagination."

"Talk about imagination," he responded, "here's a guy who claims he was born in 1753." He showed her Bob Hunt's story in the *New Haven Register*.

Karen grew up in East Haven and graduated *cum laude* from Quinnipiac College with a degree in English literature. For the past two years she was working toward a Ph.D. in English Literature at the University of Connecticut.

"I remember Professor Pellegrini," she said after she finished reading the article. "I had him for a history course at Quinnipiac. He was very regular, not flaky or anything."

"Well, Pellegrini really believes this guy. Says he has verified his birthday. Sounds like they're both *non compos mentis*," Dwight responded. "I mean how can an intelligent man, a professor, go along with something impossible like that?"

Dwight Morrow was a second-year law student at Yale. Two years ago, he and Karen found themselves seated next to each other at a concert in Wolsey Hall. They both remained in their seats during the intermission.

"Are you enjoying the concert?" Dwight asked.

"It's great. I love Brahms and Bach." They introduced themselves. When the concert ended, Dwight asked, "Would you like to join me for coffee at X and O's? It's over on Elm Street, just a few blocks. We can walk."

"Sure. That would be nice."

This led to a date the following evening and they continued to date each other exclusively ever since.

Karen read the newspaper story about Daniel.

"What do you think?" Dwight asked her. "It's weird, right?"

"I don't know," Karen told him, "but I find it very interesting. Are you finished with the paper?"

"Yeah."

She tore out the page with the story, folded it carefully and put it in her purse.

"What are you going to do?"

"I don't know," she told him. "When I find out I'll let you know."

*

"We have to do something, Joe," Linda told him one evening, after a reporter followed her home and practically demanded that she answer his questions. "The situation is getting out of hand. The kids are being harassed, I'm being hassled."

"Yeah, I know. My classes are a shambles. The students only ask questions about Daniel and smirk when I defend him."

"This certainly isn't doing your reputation...your career any good. Could they fire you?"

"Well, they could but it isn't likely. I'm a tenured professor and it would take a vote by the trustees. Maybe I should take a short sabbatical leave. You and the kids can continue school without interruption and Daniel and I could spend more time together. Maybe travel a little to show him some of the country. I'd still be on full salary. I think I'd like to write about him but, of course, none of the professional history journals would touch it."

The dean thought the idea of the sabbatical was a good one. He welcomed the opportunity to get Joseph away from the campus for a while. Joseph's classes were cancelled. His students were not surprised; they assumed that he had been fired.

*

"Our orchestra is giving a concert next week." Betsy informed Joseph after class. "Would you and Mrs. Pellegrini like to come? You could bring Daniel."

Daniel had heard Betsy practice her cello but he had never heard classical orchestral music. They found seats in the large auditorium in Buckman Center. The orchestra was already on the stage. Daniel watched intently as the student conductor appeared, the audience applauded and then became silent as the orchestra began to play. He listened, enthralled by the music of Respighi, Strauss, Tchaikovsky and Beethoven. He applauded energetically after each piece.

"For the soul of me" he effused, " I have never heard such beautiful music. So many musicians playing together."

After the concert, Daniel presented a bouquet to Betsy, an idea suggested by Linda. Betsy was delighted and kissed Daniel. The four went to a small restaurant nearby for coffee. Daniel continued to enthusiastically express his enjoyment of the music, which amused Joseph and Linda and pleased Betsy. In Joseph's car, Betsy took Daniel's arm and snuggled up to him.

"I don't care what the papers say, Daniel," she whispered. "I believe you and so does Professor Pelligrini." Daniel smiled at her.

"I thank you for that, Betsy."

*

In September, Tony was transferred to the Robinson Correctional Center. Before he left Joliet, he told Carlos, "Look man, keep your nose clean and they'll move you to a minimum security joint like I'm going to. Then it's a piece a cake to slip away. When you get out, look me up here. Then we'll go into business." Tony gave him a knowing wink and the address of a friend on the south side of Chicago.

CHAPTER 10

It was a bright, crisp Saturday, the last day in October. Daniel was leading a chestnut mare around the paddock at the Hamden Riding Stable when he heard Betsy call his name. He turned to see her sitting on the fence that enclosed the paddock.

"Hi, Daniel!" she called and waved. He was surprised and pleased to see her. He walked the horse over to where she was sitting and watched her jump down to pet the mare.

"Pray, what brings you here, Betsy?"

"I ride here whenever I can afford it," she said. "What's her name?"

"They call her Ginger and forsooth, she can be sprightly enow when she has not been ridden for a spell."

She stayed with him while he returned the horse to the stall and helped him to remove the saddle and bridle. Together they walked slowly down the dirt road that led from the stable. Daniel noticed some children costumed as witches, ghouls and skeletons, and turned questioningly to Betsy.

"Tonight's Halloween," she explained. "Those kids are getting ready for their trick or treat game." Daniel had already learned that "kids" did not refer to young goats.

"Ah, even so. I had well-nigh forgotten that this is All-Hallow's Eve."

"Did they...you have Halloween?"

"Yea, although the church elders disapproved. Children from neighboring farms gathered for a party. We carved Jack O' Lanterns from pumpkins and we bobbed for apples."

"What's that?"

"It is an amusement. Apples are floated in a tub of water and a child tries to fetch one without using his hands." They walked for a while without speaking. Betsy broke the silence.

"Daniel, is this time very different from yours?" He took a deep breath and let it out.

"Truly, Betsy, I discover this to be a most...busy and noisy place. Besides speech with my Elizabeth mornings and evenings, there was none to disturb me from morn to night. When I worked, there were only the sounds of nature, wind or thunder, the calling of birds, or a whinny or moo from the beasts, to break the stillness. But here..." he hesitated.

"Tell me," she encouraged.

"Here, there is scarce a moment of peace and quiet. Cars and trucks roar by, airplanes thunder overhead. There is the intrusion of telephones ringing. Signs are everywhere, directing, warning, forbidding, advising, selling. Voices on the radio and the TV, speaking so fast, urging one to buy, to go, or to do something...there are so many people and everything is so fast, talking, travelling, everything..." He paused, embarrassed by his outburst. Betsy took his hand and held it.

"It must be awful for you," she commiserated. "I didn't realize." He nodded. He wondered if he had spoken too freely or said too much.

*

The stories, rumors and inquiries about Daniel petered out after a few weeks. Nick and Cathy stopped complaining about teasing by their classmates who became bored with the subject of Daniel and turned to other activities. Life in the Pellegrini household returned to normal. Joseph decided to use at least a part of his sabbatical to investigate all aspects of Daniel's former life. He continued telling Daniel about the major events of the intervening years.

"Slavery was abolished in most of the industrialized northern states but the agricultural South relied upon slave labor. When Congress declared slavery to be illegal in 1860, eleven Southern states seceded from the Union to form a Confederacy and a terrible Civil War started the following year. By the time the Confederacy surrendered four years later, six hundred thousand Americans on both sides had lost their lives."

"Men should be free," Daniel said. The immense number of casualties awed him.

"We purchased Alaska from Russia in 1867 and it became our forty-ninth state. Two years after that the transcontinental railroad was completed, linking the East with California and the Pacific Coast, a distance of almost 3,000 miles."

"Now truly, that is a great distance."

The history lesson was interrupted when Cathy joined them. She soon lost interest in her father's exposition.

"Daniel," she asked, "what it was like where you came from?" Daniel looked at Joseph who nodded for him to go ahead.

"Indeed, it was very different from here...from now. We had fewer kinds of food, only what we grew, caught, hunted or slaughtered. Our garments were made by the women-folk. Most houses were much smaller and darker at night. They were cold in the winter and hot in the summer and they lacked bathrooms."

"What did you use?" the girl asked.

"Truly, there was less bathing and indeed, many people smelled the worse for it. There were privies behind the houses and..."

"What's a privy?"

"It's an outdoor toilet with no plumbing," Joseph explained. "Just a hole in the ground."

"Yuk!" Cathy said. "What else, Daniel?"

"Children often sickened and died of illnesses the doctors could not cure." Daniel thought of little Abigail and stopped.

"What else, Daniel?" Cathy persisted.

"Folk lived close to where they were born. Travel was seldom. Roads were few…" Daniel stopped again.

"I guess it wasn't much fun."

"Nay, Cathy, there was little fun but life was good. Folk worked hard, went to church, raised a family..." Daniel's eyes filled with tears and he could not continue. He excused himself and went up to his room.

Poor guy, Joseph thought. It's as though he was shipwrecked on a foreign shore with no hope of rescue or return. What would *I* do if I were in his place?

*

Whenever he had the time and was able to talk his parents into letting him use the car, Nick continued to drive Daniel to neighboring farms or to the Hamden Riding Stable. During these trips Nick often asked Daniel's opinion on subjects ranging from school events to relations with his friends and schoolmates. He confided in Daniel as one might confide in an older brother or a friendly uncle. He trusted Daniel and respected him.

On this day they were driving for a visit to a nearby farm where Daniel had made the acquaintance of the farmer. Nick was unusually quiet.

"Mayhap the cat has run off with your tongue," Daniel said. "Does ought trouble you?"

"No...yeah, I guess so. It's kind of, like a problem..."

"Methinks your father..."

"I don't want to tell Dad about it. He'd get all bent out of shape." He understood the boy's meaning.

"Ah, even so. Now truly, Nick, you may lay your troubles upon my back and I will attempt to help you if I am able."

"You won't tell Dad?"

"Fear not. May I be hanged if I disclose your secret to a living soul. You may speak freely."

"Well, I've smoked pot with a few guys after school and..."

"Smoked pot? What does that mean?"

"You know, marijuana. We turn on, get stoned. You know."

"I do not discover your meaning, young Nick. What is marijuana? Do others throw stones at you like in the Bible?" Nick laughed.

"No, marijuana is a weed, a drug like tobacco. You smoke it and it makes you high. It's harmless, but now this guy wants us to try some hard stuff like heroin. You have to inject it into your vein. He says it's a real kick but I'm afraid. You could get hooked on it and if you get caught you go to prison."

"This...guy. Is he a student too?"

"No, he just hangs around the school. He's a pusher."

"A pusher?"

"Yeah, you know. He tries to get you to use the stuff and then he sells it to you."

"What manner of man is he?"

"You mean what does he look like? Why?"

"I would persuade him to take his custom elsewhere."

"Daniel, he'd...they'd get back at me!"

"Nay, you need not be troubled. He knows me not." Nick described the man.

"He always hangs around under that big tree across from the school."

A few days later, Daniel walked the six miles to the high school. Tied around his waist and hidden under his jacket he carried a three-foot length of half-inch hemp rope that he had gotten at the Riding Stable. He recognized the pusher, a small young man dressed as Nick had described, smoking a cigarette and slouched under the large tree. There was no one else around. Daniel casually approached him.

"Pray sir, I am in need. Have you ought to sell?"

The man sullenly regarded Daniel with suspicion. He decided that Daniel was not police.

"I got all kinds of shit, man. What do you want?" Daniel's hand shot out and grabbed the man by the throat. The man's eyes grew wide, his face paled and he gasped to breathe.

"I want your companionship for a spell," Daniel told him.

"O.K. man, O.K., anything. I can't breathe!"

Daniel released his hold on the man's throat, grabbed his wrist and twisted his arm behind his back. He marched him to a clump of trees and bushes that hid them from the street, and threw him to the ground. Taking the rope from his waist, be used it to beat the man furiously on his chest, legs and back. The man yelled in pain and tried to shield himself from the blows with his hands. After a minute or two, Daniel stopped.

"Mark well this rope, thou scoundrel. I have rope aplenty. Of a certainty, when I see you next, you shall hang from yon tree. Now begone!"

The man picked himself up and ran away.

*

Two weeks later, Nick was driving Daniel to the Riding Stable.

"Remember that guy I told you about, the pusher? Well, he just, like, disappeared. So, no problem with the drugs."

"Truly, we have had enow of *that* villain," Daniel said. "But I beseech you to smoke no more of that pan." Nick laughed.

"You mean pot. O.K. Daniel, I'll stop it. It's not worth the risk."

*

Karen was intensely interested in genealogy since she read Alex Haley's *Roots* in high school. The concept and the process of locating and identifying distant ancestors was fascinating to her and she spent much of her spare time researching her family's forebears. She learned about the National Archives and Records Administration, the Library of Congress, the New England Historic Genealogical Society, the Family History Center of the Church of Jesus Christ of Latter Day Saints and a host of other sources, some of which were available on the Internet. She thought about the article describing Daniel and decided to call Joseph for more details.

"Professor Pellegrini, my name is Karen Sanders. You probably don't remember me. I took your History course about four years ago."

"What can I do for you?" Joseph asked.

"I read that story about Daniel Rowland in the *Register* and I wonder if I might ask you a few questions about it?"

"What is your specific interest in it?" Joseph asked.

"Well, I'm a graduate student in English literature at UConn and I'm interested in eighteenth century American writers, specifically Francis Hopkinson, who lived from 1737 to 1791. That's the same time that Mr. Rowland...says he came from."

"That's interesting, but how..."

"The other thing is," Karen continued, "that I'm very good at genealogical research. It's kind of a hobby and I was wondering if perhaps I might be able to find out more about Mr. Rowland."

"Hmm..." Joseph mused.

"Do you still believe he's genuine?"

"I'm afraid I do, although it goes against all reason."

"Could you give me some more details about him?" Karen asked.

"Like what?"

"His father's name, wife's name, location of his home, dates, children. You know, that stuff." Joseph told her all he could about Daniel.

"Thanks, Professor. I'll start digging."

"Please let me know if you find anything," Joseph said. "And let's keep this confidential, between you and me. O.K.?"

CHAPTER 11

Daniel came down to the kitchen to find Linda energetically cooking.

"Happy Thanksgiving, Daniel," she said, preparing stuffing from a mix.

"Thanksgiving?" he said, confused. "I am sure today is but the twenty-sixth. Methought George Washington and the Continental Congress had set the twenty-eighth of November to be Thanksgiving."

"Well, Abraham Lincoln changed that in 1863," Joseph announced, as he walked into the kitchen, "and made it a moveable feast. He decided it should be the fourth Thursday in November. Up in Canada they celebrate Thanksgiving on the second Monday in October."

"Upon my word!" Daniel said. "I am sure it is very complicated. Ah, I see that you have gotten a turkey gobbler," he added, noting the large bird defrosting in the sink.

Cathy came into the kitchen.

"How did you used to catch a turkey, Daniel?"

"Oho! You rose early and slipped into the woods while it was yet dark and hid against a large tree. Then you gave a call like an owl."

"An owl?" Linda asked.

"Even so," he explained. "Because a turkey gobbler will always answer an owl's call, and tell you where he is roosting. Then, you try to get the turkey gobbler to fly down from his perch in a tree and walk over towards you."

"How do you do that?" Cathy asked.

"You make sounds like another turkey gobbler by using a call made from the wing bone of another turkey gobbler. You must sit very still and when you see him, you aim carefully and shoot. Should you miss him, he will flee before you can shoot again. Our fowling pieces only fired once before reloading."

"What foods did you eat besides turkey?" Linda asked him.

"There was venison, turnips, potatoes, squash, and roasted ears of Indian corn. Johnny cake and pies of apple and pumpkin, and cider to wash it all down. Of course, we sat down to our dinner with friends and neighbors when all returned from church."

"How about cranberry sauce?" Linda asked.

"Of a certainty. I had well nigh forgotten. Elizabeth and I...we gathered the berries from vines growing on the marsh and dried them."

*

Daniel was lonely. Despite the friendship of Joseph and his family, he felt himself to be an outsider, a stranger in a fantastic land. The only soul that he felt comfortable with was Betsy. His feelings about her were confused. He had a vague idea that Chinese were heathens and should be avoided and that blacks were mostly slaves and were inferior to whites. He found this Jamaican half-black, half-Chinese girl to be more assertive than the women he had known but Betsy, despite her sometime pertness, had a way of putting him at ease and overcoming his reticence. He was impressed by her intelligence and he appreciated her sympathetic attitude toward him. They soon became friends and companions.

She is so different from my dear Elizabeth, he thought, yet I feel close to her too. She is like a little sister to me, nay, not so little, but sweet and kind. She is more than a sister...With the exception of the time she kissed him on the cheek when he gave her the flowers at the concert, their physical contact was limited to sometimes holding hands when walking. Occasionally, if they strolled at night, she linked her arm in his. Daniel felt such behavior was quite natural. On her part, Betsy had very warm feelings for him. She admired his complete lack of guile, his forthrightness, his gentle strength and she sympathized with his unique predicament.

*

Karen continued to search the Internet and a score of other sources without finding any record of Daniel. Then, in an old Guilford record, she found the grant of a farm to an Isaac Rowland.

I wonder if he could have been Daniel's father? She decided to search the records of the local churches and, after many weeks of fruitless hunting and probing, she found it; an obscure Madison church record:

Noah, b. Sept. 29, 1791 to Daniel and Eliz. Rowland.

Elizabeth had a son! Karen lost no time in calling Joseph with this information. He was elated; this was strong evidence that Daniel was authentic. Of course it could be claimed that anyone could look up the record and adopt Daniel's identity, but for what purpose? Joseph shared the news with Linda who was also excited. After long discussions they decided not to tell Daniel about his son. They felt it would only add to his grief.

Karen was determined to continue searching.

*

There were times when Daniel doubted the reality of what he was experiencing.

It is all a fantastic dream from which I will soon awake, he thought, and find myself back on the farm with Elizabeth.

But even in those reveries, a part of him recognized and confirmed the reality.

I could not have imagined these things.

*

"Joe," Daniel asked one evening, "Pray, when did all these marvels, these machines, come about?"

"Well," Joseph told him, "everything didn't happen all at once. What is called the Industrial Revolution started about 1875 in England and spread to Europe and America. Men saw what engines could do, how they saved physical labor. And about that time doctors began to learn that many diseases were caused by germs...bacteria...tiny plants too small to see with the naked eye. The telephone, electric lights, and the internal combustion engine, the kind that is used in our cars today, all came along. This engine is much lighter and more mobile than the steam engine. Then, the 1880's brought photography, radio, and the machine gun."

"Machine gun?"

"Yes, a weapon that can fire many times a minute. They are used by every army."

"Ah! I have seen them on the TV. They are terrible."

"The first automobile appeared in 1890 and five years later, movies. Of course, they were black and white and had no sound."

"I presume that they now have color and sound? I have a fancy to see a movie."

"Linda and I will take you, one of these days."

'We went to war with Spain in 1898." Joseph continued.

"Why? Where? How?" Daniel interrupted.

"Well, the Spanish military government in Cuba was very brutal and thousands of Cubans were imprisoned in camps where many died from disease and starvation. The Cubans demanded independence from Spain."

"Oho! Just like our colonies and the British."

"Our battleship, the *Maine,* was sunk in Havana harbor and we went to war with Spain. We destroyed most of the Spanish fleet in Manila and our troops fought the Spanish in Cuba. We won and gained Cuba, Puerto Rico and the Philippine Islands. We immediately freed Cuba, and later, the other islands."

"Indeed, I am pleased to hear of it. Men should be free." Linda came into the living room.

"Dinner is ready, gentlemen," she announced. "Please come."

*

The Parole Board convened at the Robinson Correctional Center in December to consider Tony's case. Although he had been there only four months he had been a model prisoner. The Board members were infused with Christmas spirit and they voted unanimously to grant Tony a parole. They informed him that he had to reside in Chicago, find a job, avoid consorting with known criminals, and, in addition, he was required to report regularly to a parole officer.

Tony thanked them profusely, promised to abide by all the regulations and wished them a Merry Christmas. He packed his few belongings, changed into civilian clothes and hopped a bus for Chicago. He had other plans.

*

Carlos was transferred from the Joliet prison to the Vandalia Correctional Center near Springfield. Vandalia was a minimum-security facility for prisoners who would be paroled within a year. There were no cells; the inmates lived in several dormitory-style buildings and came and went on the grounds as they wished. There were no walls and the guards were unarmed. Carlos was issued an ill-fitting set of shirts and trousers. The warden advised Carlos that if he caused any trouble he would be promptly shipped from this veritable paradise back to Joliet. A guard took Carlos aside.

"Hey man, we can make things better for you here," he told Carlos.

"Yeah? Like how?"

"We can get you clothes that fit. Someone can make your bed every day. Stuff like that."

"Yeah? What do I got to do?"

"You just get someone to send a check to my wife every month..."

Carlos had no money for that. He behaved himself. He soon learned that some of the prisoners conducted classes in arson, safe cracking, stealing cars and even murder. He attended some of these "classes" but he was now convinced that bank robbery was the crime of choice. He bided his time and, on Christmas Eve, he walked out of the Correctional Center and hitched a ride to Chicago. He was going to find Tony.

CHAPTER 12

Christmas came and with it the re-emergence of all its trappings. Streets were festooned with lights and decorations; Santas, tirelessly shaking bells, appeared on busy corners with their tripod-supported pots and Christmas music played endlessly on every radio station. Sales were advertised on television, interspersed with Christmas parades and a variety of ethnic celebrations. Shoppers reached a frenzy of last minute bargain hunting.

Joseph came home with a Christmas tree and set it up in the living room. Linda brought out decorations and a string of lights from previous years. She and Cathy enthusiastically attached them to the tree together with new tinsel. A light snow began to fall.

Daniel was overwhelmed by the magnitude of the seasonal festivities. The commercialism and the minimal religious emphasis was very different from the holiday he associated primarily with a church service that barely acknowledged Christmas. He declined repeated invitations to participate in the tree trimming. He sat and gazed out of the window, thinking of the last winter he spent with Elizabeth. He also thought of Betsy, spending the holidays with her family in Jamaica.

"Daniel," Joseph interrupted his reverie, " I have a surprise for you. Tomorrow we're all going to New York. Give you a chance to see the big city."

"Now truly, Joe, is that not a long journey?"

"Naa, we'll take the train from New Haven. It's only a two hour ride."

*

Daniel stared out of the train window and watched the towns and countryside flash by. He was awed by the sheer size and space of Grand Central Station. He shook his head in disbelief.

"I have read of huge buildings in England and in Europe. Westminster Abbey, the cathedrals and all but I never dreamed anything could be this big." They took the subway to lower Manhattan and boarded a boat to view the Statue of Liberty.

"A gift to the United States from the people of France," Joseph told them. "There is a poem on the statue, written by a Jewish woman. It goes:

Give me your tired, your poor,
Your huddled masses yearning to breathe free,
The wretched refuse of your teeming shore,
Send these, the homeless, tempest-tossed to me,
I lift my lamp beside the golden door.

My grand-parents entered America through this harbor," he added.

Their next stop was the Observation Deck of the Empire State Building. The visibility was good and Joseph was able to point out the many bridges to Daniel and describe the tunnels under the rivers. The streets were crowded with shoppers and traffic was heavy. They piled into a cab and went to Chinatown for dinner. Daniel regarded the many Chinese in the streets with suspicion but he enjoyed the food. They all had fun trying to eat with chop sticks.

They went to see the show in Radio City and afterward, viewed the giant Christmas tree in Rockefeller Center.

"Well, Daniel," Joseph asked on the train home. "What do you think?"

"Ah forsooth, it is truly a different world from the one I knew. I could never have imagined anything like this. Everything is so huge, so fast, so...I lack the words. My poor head is spinning. It is indeed a wonderment."

*

The driver of the big eighteen wheeler tractor-trailer that picked up Carlos was glad to get some company. He had been driving for eight hours and he was tired of hearing nothing but Christmas music on the radio.

You're going to Chicago, huh? You bin on the road a long time?"

"Yeah," Carlos told him.

"You got family there?"

"Yeah." This guy's a real talker.

"You hungry?"

Carlos didn't respond.

"There's a pretty good truck stop a few miles up ahead. We can grab a bite." The driver noticed Carlos' hesitancy. "It's O.K.," he assured Carlos. "I'll spring for the eats."

The diner's parking lot was full of trucks and almost all of the patrons were truck drivers. No one noticed or paid attention to Carlos' prison-issue khaki shirt and pants. A waitress seated them at a table near the counter and took their order. Half way through the meal, a State Trooper entered and sat down at the counter. Carlos stiffened and tried to shrink into the corner of the booth. The driver noticed. Carlos couldn't take his eyes off the large automatic pistol holstered on the trooper's belt. He couldn't wait to leave. He didn't know that his escape would not be noticed until bed check several hours later.

Back on the road, they drove in silence for several hours.

This guy is hot, he's wanted by the fuzz for something, the driver thought. He could be dangerous. He could be carrying a gun or a knife. I'll be glad when I'm rid of him. The truck rolled into the dark outskirts of the city.

"Where do you want to go?" he nervously asked Carlos.

"You can let me off right here," Carlos told him. The driver stopped the truck and handed Carlos a twenty-dollar bill.

"I know what it's like to be broke," he said. Carlos accepted the money.

"Thanks," he muttered and climbed down out of the cab.

The driver waved and drove off. Christ, I'm glad he's gone. Should I report him to the cops? Naa.

CHAPTER 13

Tony lived in a furnished room in a seedy section of Chicago's South side. He had a job as a dishwasher in a small restaurant and reported to his parole officer when required. Most nights he hung around a pool hall with acquaintances, most of whom had criminal records. Associating with known criminals was a violation of his parole but Tony didn't care. He was marking time waiting for Carlos. He knew that Carlos would be along soon. In the meantime he reviewed his plans for robbing banks.

Carlos found Tony's place at two o'clock on the morning of Christmas Day. Tony was not home so Carlos sat in a dark stairwell and waited. Tony showed up two hours later. He was drunk.

"Hey man, you made it!"

"Yeah," Carlos said. "You got anything to drink?"

The following day they stole a car and drove to Gary, Indiana. Late that night they held up a convenience store. Tony threatened the Pakistani clerk with a large knife he had stolen from the restaurant. He held the knife to the man's throat and ordered him to open the cash register. The clerk was paralyzed with fear. Carlos scooped up the bills and they both fled. As Tony drove, Carlos counted the money; it was four hundred and eighty-three dollars.

The clerk was too frightened to call the police immediately. When the police arrived several hours later, he was unable to give them a good description of the robbers or even to describe their car or the direction they took.

They headed East on State Route 20, avoiding the Interstate and driving at night. Tony figured that by now his parole officer had notified the police of his failure to report and Carlos knew that his escape from the correctional center had been reported. They located a small motel on a side road on the outskirts of Toledo, Ohio. The following night they went to a bar in Toledo and found a man who agreed to sell them guns. Tony bought a.38 Special Smith and Wesson revolver and Carlos got a Colt.45 automatic pistol. The guns and ammunition cost them almost all their money.

"When we going to pull a bank job?" Carlos asked. He was sitting on his bed playing with his pistol. He worked the action repeatedly, loaded the clip with cartridges, and aimed at various objects around the motel room.

"Soon," Tony told him. "First we got to get a little practice. We also need some bread."

That night they left the motel and stopped for gas at a service station in Bono, Ohio. After the attendant filled the tank, Carlos drew his gun and forced the man to open the cash register. There was only about two hundred dollars. Carlos was enraged.

"Where's the rest of it?" he demanded.

"The boss took it to deposit when he left this afternoon," the man protested.

Carlos struck him on the side of the head with the big pistol, knocking him down. He beat him repeatedly, leaving his face a bloody pulp.

"We got to find a better place," Carlos muttered as they roared away. "We only got two hundred bucks."

They continued into Pennsylvania and stayed at a motel in Elmhurst, just outside of Scranton.

"A liquor store," Tony said. "We'll find a liquor store. There's always a lot of dough in liquor stores. We both go in and do the heist." Carlos agreed. They drove into Scranton and located a liquor store in a small shopping plaza. They parked and watched customers enter and leave the store. When it appeared that there were no customers in the store, Tony and Carlos entered.

They drew their guns and Tony shouted, "This is a hold-up!"

The storeowner was behind a counter, talking to a customer they had overlooked.

"Down on the floor!" Tony yelled.

The customer and the owner quickly lay down. Carlos tried to open the register. He pounded several buttons without effect.

"Open it, you bastard!" he yelled.

The owner struggled to his feet and opened the register. Carlos hurriedly removed all the cash. He struck the owner on the head with the pistol causing him to fall to the floor unconscious.

"Let's go," Tony shouted. Carlos ran over to where the customer lay on the floor and brutally kicked him several times on his head.

"Come on!" Tony urged.

The two robbers fled the store and drove away. They hadn't noticed the surveillance cameras mounted in a corner. They left the shopping plaza and drove away at a normal speed. Carlos counted the money.

"Shit!" Carlos shouted. "Only five hundred and forty bucks. I thought you said liquor stores always had dough. What we going to do now? Where we going? When we going to do a bank?"

"I got a plan," Tony told him. "We head east and then up to Canada, see? A bank job takes some planning. We'll find the easy banks on the way. O.K.?"

"O.K.," Carlos grudgingly agreed.

They crossed into New York State and stopped in Newburgh, a small community on the western terminus of the Beacon-Newburgh Bridge that spanned the Hudson River. Two major highways, the New York State Thruway and Route 84, crossed just west of town.

"This is a good place," Tony said. "Small, quiet and they've got to have a bank here. Also, they got a lot of traffic."

They found the Reliance Savings and Loan of Newburgh on a side street and parked nearby.

"Here's the deal," Tony said. "I go in and do the heist. You stay in the car with the motor running. When I come out, we take off fast." Carlos agreed.

Tony stuffed a pillowcase, stolen from the last motel, into his pocket and entered the small bank. Two women were behind the counter and an older man sat at a desk. Tony approached one of the tellers. He drew his gun and handed her the pillowcase.

"This is a stick-up," he told her. "Do as I say and you won't get hurt. Put all your big bills in the bag. If you try to hit an alarm or anything I'll kill you."

Her eyes widened with fear. She nodded and began to fill the pillowcase with bills. Tony covered the man and the other teller with his pistol.

"Just stay put," he told them. "Hurry up," he shouted to the first teller.

Tony grabbed the filled pillowcase from her and backed to the door. A surveillance camera recorded the entire event.

"I'll shoot anyone who comes out," he yelled. He turned, ran out to the waiting car and jumped in.

"Go!" he shouted to Carlos.

They raced across the bridge on Route 84 heading for Connecticut. When they were convinced that there was no pursuit they slowed to normal traffic speed. Forty minutes later they left the main highway at Sandy Hook. A small state road led to Ansonia where they stopped at a motel.

Tony emptied the pillowcase on the bed and began to count the money.

"How much? How much?" Carlos demanded.

It took Tony almost an hour to count the money.

"We got more than twenty-six thousand," he announced. "That's..." he stopped to figure mentally. "That's thirteen thou a piece. I ain't counting the small stuff. We'll split it. Didn't I tell you that banks is the way to go?"

"Now what?" Carlos asked.

"We hole up here for a while, buy some clothes, have some fun, maybe meet some broads, until things quiet down. Then we maybe find another bank, working our way to Canada." Carlos agreed.

"Sounds good to me."

CHAPTER 14

"Everyone here seems to have those small timepieces on their wrists," Daniel observed. "I have never owned a watch and methought to buy such a one for myself if they are not too dear. Where might I find a shop that sells them?"

"Every jewelry store sells watches," Linda told him "but why not buy it on line? Joe will show you."

"On line? I do not understand..."

"On line shopping with the computer." Daniel accompanied Joseph to the den where a computer was set up.

"I have watched the children at this machine," Daniel said, "but I do not understand it. It is not TV yet..." Joseph tried to explain the computer.

"It is a machine that does many things. You can use it to write, instead of using a pen. It can send and receive mail over a telephone line. And it can connect to the Internet. The Internet is a collection of many thousands of computer networks around the world. Some are college libraries and government agencies but many are business establishments that buy and sell their products and services by means of computers like this one. I'll show you." Joseph found a site that sold watches.

"Look Daniel, this place has all kinds of watches. Pocket watches, wristwatches, all kinds, all prices. Some of these also show the date, the day of the week, the phase of the moon, and some are chronometers, you know, with stop watches. Some are water-proof. If you see something you like, we can check the price and order it with a few clicks of the mouse. It will be delivered in a few days by the postman."

"It is truly a wonder! What other things can be purchased with this computer?"

"You name it. Clothing, food, medicines, even cars. Do you see a watch you like?"

"Many of these are far too fancy for such as me. What are the prices, Joe?"

"There's a big range, from about sixty dollars to many thousands."

Daniel selected a wristwatch for sixty dollars. When it was delivered, he paid Joseph from the money he got from the sale of his coins. He consulted his watch frequently, admiring the sweep second hand.

"Even your timepieces are quick," he observed to Joseph. "In my Guilford, if a man owned a watch and he wished to know the time, he stopped what he was doing and took his watch from his pocket, opened the case to look and then closed it again and returned it to his pocket. Here you have only to glance at your wrist."

*

Karen spent much of her free time searching for Daniel's descendents. She found that Daniel's son, Noah, married in 1817 and moved to New Haven. He and his wife had a daughter, Anne, who died when she was two, and a son, James. James married in 1844 and had three sons: Peter, Ralph, and John. Karen found that Peter Rowland moved to Cleveland, Ohio in 1880 and married Helen. They had two daughters, Emily and Rose, and in 1885, a son, Leonard. There was no further record of Ralph or John, but she continued her search. With the exception of Linda, Joseph told no one of Karen's searching or of her findings.

*

Betsy was back from her holiday in Jamaica. She missed Daniel and told her parents about him. To her surprise, her father was not overly concerned with Daniel's unexplained arrival from colonial times. He simply accepted that as a wonder and told his daughter that Daniel seemed to be a good man.

Betsy was in her final semester and her course load was light. She had ample free time and she spent much of it with

Daniel. They took long walks when the weather was fair and spent evenings together in the Pellegrini living room.

"What are you going to do, Daniel?" she asked him one day, after they walked in silence for a long time.

"I would to Heaven return to my old life, dear Betsy," he said with a deep sigh, "but I fear that will never be. Whatever brought me here has left me like a piece of driftwood cast up upon the sand and here I must remain." He paused for a few moments. "But I cannot continue to live on Joe and Linda's largesse. I must find work."

"But what can you do?" She was about to tell him that he would be welcome to stay with her parents in Jamaica but she stopped herself. She realized that such an arrangement would be unacceptable to him.

"Now truly there is only one occupation that I know and that is farming. Nick has kindly driven me around to farms close by. One of the farmers, Harmon Platt, has offered me work...a job. He has taught me to drive a tractor and I have been practicing in his barn. I could start in the Spring. I have well-nigh decided to go with him."

"That's great, Daniel!" she responded enthusiastically. "Where will you live?"

"Ah, I know not. I shall discuss this with Joe."

That evening after dinner, Daniel broached the subject of his working with Joseph and Linda. They were both very impressed with his initiative and his newly acquired ability to drive a tractor.

"Well, I will say that I would prefer to be hitching up my Nell," Daniel told them with a smile, "and the tractor is noisy and smelly, but it is truly faster than my horse. And now, dear friends, I can no longer continue to avail myself of your kind hospitality and generosity. Pray counsel me as to where I may find lodgings of my own."

"Don't go, Daniel," Cathy pleaded. "Stay with us." Nick chimed in, "Come on Daniel, stay."

"You're welcome to stay with us as long as you like," Linda told him. "We enjoy having you."

Daniel blushed with pleasure at the warmth of their response. He threw an arm around each of the children and hugged them to his chest.

"Truly, I have been fortunate indeed to have such friends but I must begin to stand on my own feet in this new world."

"May I ask what salary the farmer offered you?" Joseph asked.

"His offer was most generous. He said that my wages would be one hundred and fifty dollars a week."

"That's no princely sum. It's less than minimum wage but I guess its O.K. for a start. You'll be hard put to pay rent and have some left over for food. Your best bet would be to find a boarding house near the farm."

"A bawdy house?" Daniel protested. "Not for the world! Nay, I could not."

Joseph and Linda burst out laughing. Nick and Cathy looked puzzled.

"No," Joseph explained. "A boarding house, a rooming house, where you would have your own room and take your meals together with the owner and the other guests."

"Ah," Daniel nodded in understanding. "An inn."

"We'll check it out," Joseph told him.

"Daniel," Linda asked, "do you still have that twenty-five hundred dollars from the sale of your coins?"

"Ah forsooth, the money lies under my bed."

"That's not very safe. You should put it in a bank where it could earn interest for you."

Daniel looked confused.

"Interest is what the bank pays you for the use of your money, usually about four or five percent. You can withdraw as much of it as you need whenever you want," she explained. "I'll take you to our bank here in Hamden and help you to open an account." Daniel nodded agreement.

*

"When we going to hit another bank?" Carlos asked. "This dough ain't going to last forever."

"I been checking around," Tony said. "There's a little burg just up the road from here with a couple a banks. We're going to hit one soon."

"What place is that?"

"It's called Hamden."

CHAPTER 15

Daniel often thought about the inexplicable event that had wrenched him from his own time. Was it a freakish stroke of nature or the deliberate act of some supernatural being...God or the Devil? If it *was* intentional, was it capricious or was there a purpose? What could the purpose be?

Am I supposed to be some kind of a messenger from my time? What could the message be? What can I, an unlettered farmer, tell these folk? Their lives are so complicated, so hurried. I could only think to tell them to slow down and pay more heed to things like caring for each other, and family and pride and satisfaction with their work and...Oh, it is surely prideful of me to imagine that *I* have been selected as a messenger. It is sinful. I will accept my fate, whatever that may be. But I will never become as they are. I could not. I will remain as I am.

Daniel never mentioned these thoughts to anyone, not even to Betsy. He had abandoned any hope of returning to his own time and he was content to exist on the fringe of present-day society, observing human activities but remaining detached and isolated.

I wish I could contribute some bit of wisdom or advice, he thought, but whenever I describe things as I knew them, my friends invariably tell me that such things have been improved upon or discarded.

*

Joseph cut short his sabbatical and returned to teaching. His students still asked about Daniel. He didn't know what to tell them. How could he explain the unexplainable? Karen's genealogical research confirmed the validity of Daniel's existence in 1790, but not in 1998. Joseph wanted to write a paper about Daniel for one of the history journals but he knew that none of them would accept it. It would be branded as fantasy or science fiction.

*

Karen continued her exploration for Daniel's descendants. She discovered that his great-great grandson, Leonard Rowland, born in Cleveland in 1885, served in the U.S. Army in World War I as a sergeant in an infantry company. Leonard's regiment was sent to France where he was wounded in action. He was sent home to an army hospital in New Haven, Connecticut. After his discharge from the army in 1918, Leonard remained in New Haven where he married Dorothy in 1920. Their son Roger was born the following year. Roger attended Yale University for two years, then left to join the Navy in World War II. After the war, Roger returned to Yale to graduate from the Law School in 1950 and practiced law in New Haven. Karen made no attempt to contact Roger but she told Dwight and Joseph of her findings.

*

Betsy's feelings for Daniel, initially admiration, ripened through affection to more tender and romantic ones. She often held his arm close to her as they walked.

"Daniel," she asked him one afternoon, "have you ever thought about getting married?" He shook his head sadly.

"Ah, Betsy, I could not. In my mind and my heart I am still married to Elizabeth even though she..." Her eyes filled with tears.

"I love you, Daniel." She hugged his arm to her breast.

"And I love you," he told her. "Be my friend, my sister."

"I will always be your friend."

*

Daniel's spirits rose with the first signs of spring. He eagerly anticipated working on the farm. Joseph found a room for him in the home of an older widowed lady. The rent was very reasonable and the house was within walking distance of the farm where Daniel would be working. The lady was very happy to have the company of a man who was a paying boarder. She indicated that Daniel could take his meals with her whenever he wished. She was intrigued by his quaint speech. He moved in with his few belongings, accompanied by Betsy and the Pellegrini family. Linda drew him aside.

"What are you going to do with your money?" she whispered. "You can't keep it under your bed here. It's not safe."

"For the soul of me I had forgotten about it," he told her. "Would you keep the money for me until we can go to the bank?"

"O.K., Daniel but let's do it soon. I could pick you up and take you to the bank next Saturday."

"I would deem that a favor, Linda. I shall be ready."

*

Mrs. Driscoll, Daniel's landlady, was frail but alert and sprightly. Daniel often took his meals with her. She enjoyed cooking for him; her background was German and she sometimes cooked German dishes that he enjoyed. She had been a schoolteacher and she still spoke as if she were in front of her first-grade class. She and Daniel had long conversations about how elementary education had changed. He was surprised to hear that prayer and religion had been banned from public schools by the Supreme Court.

"It's the separation of church and state, you know," she explained, "but I just can't see how reading one of the psalms or a moment of silent prayer can do any harm. And the children are so aggressive now, some are even violent and assault their teachers. Not the first-graders, of course." She smiled in remembrance. "My classes were always well behaved." She paused and dabbed a handkerchief to her eyes. "I miss them."

Daniel walked the few miles to the farm every day. Working on Harmon Platt's farm was a pleasure for him. He eagerly anticipated each day's labor and the ensuing weariness each evening. He immersed himself totally in the work and he readily accepted the disparity between the traditional agricultural practices he knew and modern farm machinery and methods.

This is the work I fancy, he thought, but it is a pity that I cannot be doing it on my own farm.

When the weather was foul he remained in the house reading or watching television. Weekends he did chores around the house, unasked but very much appreciated. He mowed the lawn, split a cord of wood and undertook to paint the small house. He experienced more pleasure in those things that had not changed, nature and human relationships, than in the modern marvels he encountered. He delighted in children, animals, the rain and snow and the smell of the soil.

Daniel was very grateful for Joseph's friendship and protection. He considered Linda and the children like his own family, a family he would never have, and Betsy.... Betsy was his most intimate and constant companion. He admired her vigor, her sincerity and her forthrightness. He thought of her tenderly. She was like a dear, sweet sister.

*

How we going to do this one?" Carlos asked.

"It's a piece a cake," Tony explained. "We both go in. There's one guard, an old guy,he don't carry no heat. You cover him and any people that's inside. I go to the window and get the dough. Then we split and head for Canada."

CHAPTER 16

Linda honked her horn in front of Daniel's house at nine-thirty on Saturday morning. Cathy was with her.

"Get in, Daniel," she called as he appeared at the door. She handed him a large roll of bills. "Here's your money. You should count it to see that it's all there."

"Nay, I do not deem that to be necessary," he told her with a smile.

"O.K., then. Let's go." They drove into Hamden. Cathy, in the rear seat, eagerly told Daniel about her selection for the girl's soccer team.

The Hamden Home Savings Bank was located on a quiet street off the main road in the downtown district. There was a small parking area with a drive-through window. Linda and Cathy with Daniel in tow entered the bank. Inside, there were two tellers; a young woman who was taking care of both the drive-through and inside windows, and an older black woman at the second window who was helping a young woman carrying an infant.

The guard, an older man with silver hair, recognized Linda.

"Good morning, Mrs. Pelligrini," he smiled. "Hi, Cathy."

"Good morning, Ed. How are you?"

"I'm just fine. How can I help you today?" he asked.

"This gentleman would like to open an account here,"

The guard led them to a young man seated at a nearby desk. A small sign on the desk read "Roberto Salazar, Manager."

"Please have a seat," he started. "What can I..."

At that moment, Carlos and Tony burst into the bank with guns drawn.

"Don't nobody move!" Carlos shouted.

Tony went to the first teller's window and pointed his gun at her face. Her eyes widened in fear.

"Give me all the big bills," he demanded.

She nodded and reached into the cash drawer and handed him a package of bait money, a pack of two thousand singles with twenty-dollar bills at each end. Tony grabbed the package, examined it and started to open it. The package exploded with a loud pop scattering the bills on the floor and spraying purple dye all over his face and clothes.

"Shit!" he shouted. He turned his gun toward the teller but she ducked beneath the window where she cowered, shaking with fear. He examined the bills scattered on the floor and saw that most of them were singles. He became enraged and peered down at the teller where she huddled on the floor.

"You bitch!" he screamed. "I told you, get me the big bills." The young woman, shaking uncontrollably, got to her feet and began to hand all the cash to him.

Ed, the guard, took a several steps toward the first teller. Carlos fired at him. The heavy slug struck him in the shoulder, knocking him down. The sound of the shot was deafening in the small bank. Cathy screamed and clung to Linda. Daniel and the manager sat frozen. After a few moments, the guard began to moan in pain. Daniel stood up.

"Sit down, you," Carlos ordered. Daniel was outraged.

"Now truly, yon wounded man is sorely in need of help," he said. He walked over to where the guard lay.

"Don't move! Leave him alone," Carlos yelled.

Daniel ignored him. He knelt by the guard and inspected his wound. It was bleeding profusely. Daniel tore a piece off of his shirttail and applied it to the wound. Carlos aimed his pistol at Daniel and was about to fire when the black teller interrupted.

"I can't hold my hands up any more," she announced loudly. "I've got bad arthritis."

"Don't move or I'll kill you," Carlos shouted, swinging his gun from Daniel and pointing it at her.

"O.K., O.K.," she told him. Without moving her head, she strained her eyes to search for the silent alarm button on the floor of her cage. She located it and carefully began to extend her shaking foot toward the alarm but she found that with her arms raised she was unable to reach the button.

"I got to put my hands down. I can't help it." She lowered her hands to her desk. The baby began to cry.

"Shut that kid up!" Tony yelled.

Moving very slowly, the teller slightly shifted her position forward. Now she was able to move her foot further. She prayed that she wouldn't slip or be noticed. She glanced down again, located the alarm button, carefully moved her foot over it and pressed it. Tony walked over to her window. For a moment she thought he saw her pressing the alarm and her heart seemed to stop. He pointed his pistol at her head. He looked terrifying with his purple stained face.

"Give me all the big bills and no tricks," he told her, "or I'll blow your brains out."

"O.K." She opened her drawer and began to hand him bills. Her hands were shaking so badly she could hardly pick up the money.

Carlos was keeping everybody covered when the first of several police sirens began to sound on the street.

"Cops!" Carlos shouted, as if an explanation of the sirens was necessary. He and Tony backed together to the center of the bank covering everyone with their guns. Tony clutched a bag of money.

"Everybody stay where you are," he commanded.

A few moments later a loud voice, amplified by a bull horn, announced, "This is the police. The bank is surrounded. You have five minutes to come out with your hands up." More sirens sounded. Carlos screamed an obscenity to the street.

For the next ten minutes no one moved. Nothing happened. The silence was suddenly punctuated by the ringing of the telephone on the manager's desk. No one moved. The phone continued to ring.

"Answer it!" Tony shouted at last. Mr. Salazar picked up the phone.

"Hello?" he said hoarsely. He listened for a moment. He looked at Tony.

"It's the police. They want to talk to you." Tony grabbed the phone from him.

"Yeah?" He listened for a minute.

"We got women and children in here. You know, hostages. You come in and they get it." He slammed the phone down.

"What're we going to do?" Carlos asked.

"Shut up. I got to think." The phone rang again. Tony grabbed it.

"Yeah?" He listened intently. "Call me in an hour." He broke the connection.

The baby began to cry again. The mother rocked it in her arms trying to comfort and quiet it.

"Shush," she whispered to the child. "Shush."

The phone rang again. Tony seized it.

"Yeah?" There was a pause. "We got four women and two kids. I told you, call in an hour."

Tony and Carlos conferred. The talked animatedly in low voices, gesticulating wildly. Every few minutes they looked around at their hostages pointing their guns at them. The baby continued to cry, now louder and more insistent.

"Can't you shut that kid up?" Tony yelled at the young mother.

"I can't help it'," the woman said. "She's hungry. Her bottle is outside in the car." She began to sob and rocked the baby vigorously.

A tense hour passed. The two tellers stood motionless behind their windows. Linda, Cathy and Mr. Salazar huddled around his desk. Daniel knelt by the guard on the floor, trying to stanch the bleeding by pressing on his wound. The baby's crying became more strident. Daniel became more and more incensed; he couldn't imagine ignoring a hungry infant. He stood up.

"Where the hell you think you're going?" Tony yelled at him.

"I beseech you, permit me to fetch some milk for that hungry child. Fear not, I shall return."

"You take one more step and I'll blow you away," Tony told him. Daniel tore open his shirt to expose his chest.

"Shoot then, you villain," he shouted. "I will bring milk for that infant. He turned and strode purposefully towards the door.

"Daniel," Linda called. "Please listen to them! Don't make them angry. They're killers."

Carlos raised his automatic and took aim at Daniel's retreating back. Tony pushed Carlos' gun arm down.

"What are you doing?" Carlos protested. "He's getting away!"

"Let him go. He's just a crazy creep. He's trouble. He won't come back. We don't need him. We got the women and the kids."

Daniel appeared at the bank door and walked toward the line of police vehicles. Twenty guns were raised and aimed at him. The Hamden police chief cautiously emerged from behind a car and walked forward to meet him. A sheriff and a captain of the state police joined them.

"What's going on in there? Who are you? Has someone been shot?"

"My name is Daniel Rowland. I'm from Guilford. There are two robbers in there. My friend Linda and her daughter Cathy are in there and a woman with a babe in arms. There are also two ladies and a gentleman who work in the bank and the guard who lies wounded on the floor."

"How badly is he wounded?"

"He was struck in the shoulder. He has lost much blood."

"Why did they let you out?" the police chief asked.

"Forsooth, they did not let me. I came out to fetch some milk for the child who is crying from hunger."

"You mean you just walked out? Just like that?" the sheriff asked. Daniel nodded.

"You aim to go back in there?"

"Even so," Daniel told him. "Methinks a little water and some bandages for the wounded man would not be amiss."

"You're crazy."

Ambulances and vans from several TV stations were parked nearby and a crowd of spectators was held back by police. A package of six nursing bottles with milk and several bottles of water were quickly produced from a nearby store. They gave these to Daniel together with some sterile gauze bandages. He thanked them and walked swiftly back into the bank.

Tony and Carlos were startled by Daniel's reappearance.

"Come here, you," Carlos commanded, aiming his gun at Daniel. Daniel ignored him and gave the milk bottles to the mother.

"Thank you, sir," she whispered.

"I told you to come here," Carlos yelled. Daniel continued to ignore him. He walked over to the wounded guard and examined the wound. The bleeding had stopped. He gently removed the torn piece of shirttail and replaced it with a clean gauze bandage. The guard moaned. Daniel lifted the man's head and gave him some water.

"You better search him," Tony called out. Carlos was enraged. He walked up behind Daniel and rammed his gun in Daniel's back.

"Stand up, you bastard," he screamed. Daniel stood up. As Carlos was searching him Daniel suddenly whirled around with his right arm extended to a large fist and struck Carlos a terrific blow on the side of his head. Carlos went down like a felled ox, unconscious, dropping his gun with a clatter. Daniel quickly bent to retrieve the weapon when Tony fired at him. Daniel felt a terrific blow to his chest as the bullet struck him. He managed to raise the unfamiliar weapon and aim it at Tony. Tony squeezed the trigger of his gun again but his pistol failed to fire. He pulled the trigger again and again but nothing happened. Daniel staggered to his feet and aimed Carlos' gun at Tony. Tony dropped his gun and raised his hands.

"Don't shoot!" he yelled at Daniel. "Please don't shoot." he pleaded.

Daniel remained standing, clutching his chest with his left hand but still covering Tony with the pistol.

The phone rang. Mr. Salazar picked it up and listened for a moment.

"You can come in now. It's all over. I'm the manager. Please hurry, we have two wounded men here."

Moments later the police charged in with guns drawn. Carlos was beginning to stir. He and Tony were handcuffed and swiftly led away. Daniel handed the gun to a nearby police officer and collapsed. Paramedics rushed in with stretchers for the wounded men and carried them to waiting ambulances. The tellers hugged each other in jubilation. Mr. Salazar remained sitting in his chair as if dazed. The woman with the baby was weeping with relief. TV crews moved into the bank and were interviewing the tellers and Mr. Salazar.

Joseph heard of the robbery on the radio while he was driving to the market. He quickly diverted to the bank, rushed in and hugged Linda and Cathy.

"Are you O.K.? Did you get hurt?"

"We're fine, Joe," Linda told him. "Just a little shaky."

"Daniel was shot, Daddy," Cathy sobbed. "They took him away in an ambulance."

A man approached Joseph. He looked vaguely familiar.

"Professor Pellegrini, you probably don't remember me. I'm Bob Hunt, the reporter for *The New Haven Register.* I interviewed you and Mr. Rowland some time ago."

"I remember you. You wrote a story that got me into trouble with the college."

"I'm sorry Professor, but that was the way I saw it. Can you tell me anything about what happened here?"

"I have no comment," Joseph told him. He turned to Linda and Cathy. "Let's go."

Betsy broke away from the crowd and rushed over to find Daniel but his ambulance was already speeding away with its siren screaming.

Please, she prayed. Please don't let him die.

*

Daniel was rushed to the operating room. He was clinging to life. The bullet had punctured his left lung, and damaged his spleen and left kidney. He had lost a lot of blood. The surgeons worked on him for more than six hours. He was moved to the surgical intensive care unit in critical condition. Joseph and Betsy were waiting outside the operating room and they hurried over to question the weary surgeon.

"How is he? Is he going to make it?" The doctor looked grim.

"He lost a lot of blood and he's still in shock," he told them, "but he's a strong young man. If he survives the next twenty-four hours, his chances are good."

Betsy was not permitted to see Daniel. She waited outside of the ICU that night and much of the next day, anxiously hoping for news of his condition. Joseph found her dozing on a couch in the waiting room and insisted on taking her down to the hospital cafeteria for some food and coffee. They cornered the surgeon as he came out of the ICU. This time he was smiling.

"He's doing better than we expected. His blood pressure has stabilized and if he continues to improve we'll move him to a room in a day or so."

"Can we see him?"

"Not just yet. He's still heavily sedated and he needs rest. Soon."

Joseph took Betsy home. She was exhausted. Two days later Daniel was transferred to a private room and visitors were permitted for brief periods. He opened his eyes briefly and smiled at Betsy but then lapsed into sleep again.

Betsy returned the next day to find the room was empty. She panicked. A sympathetic nurse explained that Daniel had developed a fever and was found to have an infection. He was taken back to surgery and was now in the ICU again in critical condition. Betsy raced up to the ICU and camped there until she recognized Daniel's surgeon and rushed over to him.

"The bullet also nicked his small intestine which we didn't know about when we operated on him. We've repaired that but he has developed peritonitis and is very shocky. We've got him on high-dose antibiotics and he's had several transfusions. It's too early to tell."

Daniel remained in the ICU for a week. Betsy accosted every nurse and doctor that came out of the unit but got little information. Joseph came every day and sat with her for hours. On the seventh day they were both excited to see Daniel being wheeled out of the unit and taken again to a private room.

CHAPTER 17

HAMDEN BANK ROBBERS FOILED BY COLONIAL VISITOR

By Tom Hunt

HAMDEN, CT.-Two bank robbers got more than they bargained for yesterday when they held up the Hamden Home Savings Bank. They shot the guard, Ed Russo, 67, seriously wounding him. One of the customers present was Daniel Rowland, 36. Mr. Rowland refused to be cowed by the robbers and proceeded to care for the wounded man. He defied their threats, walked out of the bank to get some milk for the baby of another customer and then returned to the besieged bank to care for Mr. Russo. Mr. Rowland knocked out one of the hold-up men but was shot by the other robber. Despite his serious wound, Mr. Rowland forced the second robber to surrender. Both wounded men were taken to Yale-New Haven Hospital where Mr. Rowland, is listed in critical condition. Mr. Russo was listed in serious condition but is expected to recover.

Mr. Rowland stated in an interview last year that he was born in Guilford in 1753 and lived on a farm there.

*

Dwight read the story about Daniel and the bank robbery in Hamden in the *New Haven Register* and phoned Karen to tell her about it.

"Isn't that the guy whose family you've been researching all this time?"

"Yes, Oh yes," she cried. "Thanks, Dwight." She lost no time in calling Joseph.

"Professor Pellegrini, I heard about Daniel and the bank robbery."

"Yes," Joseph told her. "Wasn't that something? He's really quite a guy. He's still in the hospital. He was badly wounded."

"I've got to meet him." Karen said "After all the work I've been doing locating his descendants...and now this. I must meet Daniel."

"O.K.," Joseph told her, "but I don't want to tell him about his family...yet. Let's wait until he recovers."

"Fine. Please call me when he's out of the hospital. I'll be coming with my boyfriend, Dwight. He's a law student."

*

Daniel's recovery from his wound and the subsequent surgeries was slow. Over the ensuing weeks he was weaned from intravenous nutrition to taking food by mouth. He still required pain medication and antibiotics but he was able to walk to the bathroom with the assistance of a nurse. Betsy visited every day. She saw that he had little appetite for the hospital food and she brought him small portions of the Chinese, Indian or Thai food that he enjoyed. They talked of her home in Jamaica and she suggested that Daniel might like to visit her island and convalesce there. Often she sat by his bed for hours, quietly holding his hand as he drifted in and out of sleep.

After several weeks, Mr. Salazar, the bank manager, came to visit accompanied by Joseph, both tellers and the young mother who had been a customer. They all came after work to see Daniel and they greeted him warmly. Mr. Salazar shook his hand.

"I thought you'd be glad to know that Ed, the guard, has been discharged from the hospital. He's recovering nicely and should be back to work in a few weeks. Also, Mr. Rowland, the bank management wants to do something to express our gratitude for your actions during the robbery. We will be adding a thousand dollars to your account balance. And the bank is picking up your hospital expenses." The women clapped their hands but Daniel shook his head.

"Nay, not for the world. You need not reward me. I sought only to do what needed to be done. I dare not accept."

"The money is already in your account. Please, Mr. Rowland, that's what we want to do. Let's say no more about it."

"It's O.K., Daniel," Joseph added, "It's what they want to do." Daniel drummed his fingers on the bed and shook his head.

"Even so," he said, "I do not deem it to be the right thing." The young mother came to the bedside.

"And I want to thank you so much for what you did for my baby. You were so brave. She's only three months old."

Daniel nodded. "I had a little girl once, a long time ago." He patted the woman gently on the shoulder as she bent to kiss his cheek.

A few days later Harmon Platt came to see him. He brought a get-well card from Mrs. Driscoll and some cookies that she baked for him.

"How're you feeling?" the farmer asked jovially. Without waiting for an answer he continued.

"Planted an acre of broccoli the other day. Could have used you on the transplanter." Daniel smiled.

"I read about you and that bank robbery in town," Harmon continued. "I guess you really showed those bastards." Daniel nodded.

"What's all this stuff about you being born in 1753?"

Daniel related the series of events. Harmon listened with a doubting expression on his face.

"You don't expect me to believe that, do you? That'd make you more'n two hundred years old and you don't look much older than thirty to me. Anyways, what became of your farm?" Daniel shrugged and shook his head.

"I know not, friend Harmon. We went back. There's naught there now."

"You should find out what happened to it," the farmer said. "It could be worth some money to you. Get yourself a lawyer. Not that I believe one word of this bullshit," he added

*

Daniel was gradually growing stronger. His wounds were healing, he required less medication for pain and he looked forward to leaving the hospital. Joseph was a frequent visitor; he usually brought news of the doings of Nick, Cathy and Linda but inevitably their conversation turned to the differences between Daniel's time and the present.

"Nothing mattered more than the family," Daniel told him one afternoon. "It was a very sedate world. Our home life was the main thing. People were more civil then."

"What do you mean?" Joseph asked.

"Well, today people pass you on the street without so much as a glance, let alone a 'Good Day' and many say to you 'Have a nice day' and turn quickly away. They do not really mean it."

"What else, Daniel?"

"Everything is so fast, Joe. I find it hard to keep up. Folk speak fast, travel fast and rush hither and yon...it is crowded and noisy. Your life is truly easier than ours with all those machines but I must say that I think many of your conveniences, like telephones and TV's, are distractions from life's pleasures."

"Which pleasures?"

"Well, time to just sit and think, watch the sun go down, good friends, companionship, true feelings. Everyone here has a consuming need for news and entertainment. Violence...and sex fascinate you so that there is little time or interest in each other. Everyone thinks only of wealth and material goods with scarce a thought of..." Daniel stopped, embarrassed by his outburst. "Pray forgive me, good Joe. I should not have spoken so to one who has been the truest of friends."

"That's O.K., Daniel. I never realized you felt this way. But didn't people in your time hanker for news? Didn't they enjoy entertainment?"

"Even so. Yet those things were but a small part of our lives. News was seldom and mostly by word of mouth. And entertainment..." A nurse stuck her head into the room.

"You're going home, Daniel," she announced cheerfully. "The doctor is discharging you tomorrow."

"You're going to stay with us until you're back on your feet," Joseph said. "You're not well enough to live at Mrs. Driscoll's."

"Thank you, Joe. Forsooth, I do not yet have my strength back."

"Good. Betsy will pick you up tomorrow. Linda and the kids will be pleased. She's making the spaghetti and meatballs that you like and there are some people who want to meet you."

*

Joseph lay in bed that evening but sleep eluded him.

I really believe that Daniel is genuine, he thought, and the means of his coming is a mystery to him and to us. But why did he come...or was he sent? I'm sure he doesn't know. Other cultures have had visitors from a distant time or place...heroes, saviors or gods. Quetzalcoatl, the Feathered Serpent of the Aztecs who created fire, discovered maize, cured disease and brought music and dance. The Mayans knew him as Kuculcan. And there was Hiawatha of the Iroquois and other North American tribes, who brought corn, peace and picture writing to his people. The Anglo-Saxons had Beowulf and we Christians had Jesus...Is Daniel some kind of messenger like them? There's nothing heroic about him but he's a very nice guy...

*

Linda was looking forward to Daniel's visit. She hadn't seen him since the bank robbery. She was in the kitchen preparing dinner when Joseph looked in.

"Joe, I've been thinking about that girl Karen coming over tonight with all that information about Daniel's family. I think we ought to tell him about...you know, about his son."

"We've discussed that, Lin, and we decided that it would just add to his grief."

"Yes, I know but I don't think we should keep that from him. He has a right to know that he had a son. I feel very strongly about that."

"Maybe you're right. After all, what difference could it make in his situation? I...we can tell him when he gets here."

*

Cathy ran to greet Daniel with a big hug that made him wince from his barely healed wounds. Nick followed close behind her.

"Hi Daniel," he called with a big smile. "Hi, Betsy."

"Hello, young Nick," Daniel responded. "Methinks you must have grown another inch or two since we last met. Is all well with you?" Nick's eyes met Daniel's.

"Everything is fine, Daniel." Daniel nodded and smiled. They had their secret understanding.

Linda kissed Daniel and welcomed Betsy. Joseph brought the two into the living room.

"Sit down, Daniel. Can I get you a drink?"

Daniel declined. He sat on the couch between Betsy and Linda.

"I've got some important news for you, Daniel," Joseph began.

"I trust it is good news," Daniel responded with a smile.

"This girl...young woman, Karen, has been searching old records about your family. She's coming over this evening.

Well, she discovered that...you and Elizabeth had a son. His name was Noah..."

Daniel sat bolt upright, his eyes widened.

"A son. We had a son." Tears filled his eyes. Linda took his hand and Betsy took his arm. "We had a little boy," Daniel seemed to announce to the group. Tears ran down his cheeks but he was smiling. "Noah. Yes, a fine name. Pray, Joe, what ought can you tell me of my son Noah?"

The doorbell interrupted. It was Karen and Dwight. Joseph introduced the pair to everyone. Karen was intrigued by Daniel's way of speaking.

"Did you by any chance know Francis Hopkinson?" she asked him. "He was a writer,"

"Nay, Miss Karen, I did not have the pleasure of knowing him but our school master told us of him and read to us a story that he wrote. I recollect it was something about an old farm, a new farm and some nobleman who..."

"Yes, yes," Karen broke in excitedly. "That was his *A Pretty Story*. Those were allegories to represent England, America and King George the Third. I'm writing my dissertation on Hopkinson. Not very many people, even English majors, ever heard of him." She looked knowingly at Dwight.

After dinner everyone returned to the living room. Joseph told Karen that Daniel knew about Noah.

"Pray, Miss Karen, I beseech you, can you tell me ought of Noah?"

"Please call me Karen. I'll tell you everything I've learned." She glanced at Joseph who nodded for her to go ahead.

"Your son, Noah, married in 1817 and moved to New Haven. They had a daughter, Anne, and a son, James. I'm afraid that's all I was able to learn about Noah, but I..."

"Alas, that is precious little."

"That was a long time ago, Daniel," Joseph said quietly, "and he's gone now."

"Even so, it is a wretched thing that he is dead and I still live." Everyone was silent for a few moments. Karen took a deep breath and continued.

"Your grandson, James, married in 1844. He lived in New Haven and raised three sons, Peter, Ralph, and John." Daniel listened with rapt attention. Karen continued.

"I was unable to find anything further about Ralph or John but Peter Rowland moved to Cleveland, Ohio in 1880. He had a son Leonard. Leonard enlisted in the Army during World War I; he was wounded in France and sent to a military hospital in New Haven. After he was discharged, he remained in New Haven where he met and married Dorothy. A year later, they had a son, Roger. Roger went to Yale and served in the Navy during World War II. He graduated from Yale Law School. He lives in New Haven with his wife and two sons, James and Peter. Roger is your great-great-great grandson."

"You astonish me," Daniel said. "For the soul of me, I do not know what to believe. It is all...unnatural. My head is spinning. I dare not think on it all at once. I am most grateful to you, Miss...Karen, for your laboring on my behalf. May I presume to ask what became of my...our farm?"

"I really don't know. Your wife, Elizabeth, passed away in 1828. Noah moved to New Haven eleven years before that. I don't know, Daniel." Daniel drummed his fingers on his thigh.

"I have a fancy to learn what became of the farm. My friend, Farmer Platt, has advised me to consult a lawyer and I have well nigh determined to do so."

Dwight listened attentively to Karen's explanations and watched Daniel's reactions. The whole story was beyond belief yet the evidence of Daniel's authenticity was very persuasive.

"Perhaps I can help you, Mr. Rowland. I'm not a lawyer yet but I am a law student. Maybe Karen and I could investigate and find out what happened to your farm."

"Forsooth, I would be your grateful servant, sir, were you to discover the fate of my farm. I have some money and I can pay."

"It's too early to talk of payment. Let's see what we can come up with."

On their way home, Karen asked, "What do you think? Do you believe him? His speech pattern is authentic and he knew about Francis Hopkinson."

"I don't know what to believe. But if he's my client, I must believe him. Let's see what we turn up."

CHAPTER 18

The New Haven Register reported on the trial of Carlos and Tony. Carlos was found guilty of attempted murder. He and Tony were also found guilty of armed robbery. They received long prison sentences after which they will be extradited in turn to Indiana, Ohio and New York to face trial in those states for armed robbery. They will eventually be returned to Illinois to serve the remainder of their original sentences.

*

"Dwight, I think I found it," Karen said excitedly. She pointed to a page in a large book, marked "Land Titles, 1740-1760." They were in the Guilford Town Clerk's office. Dwight went over to look at the page which, like the other pages in the book, was a photostat of the original document and was black and almost unreadable. Together, they were able to make out the handwritten entry:

> *Granted to Isaac Rowland, November 1757, 18 acres in the Hammonassett meadows. Ye land lies on ye east side of the river. Southeast corner by a black oak marked 68 rods north of the Totoket path and 28 and one half rods east of the bank of ye river. From thence a northerly leg of 59 rods and three feet adjoining ye land of Thomas Griswold. An easterly leg of 54 rods to ye edge of Sunnybrook Pond to ye land of Peter Hull by a rock marked and thence southerly 64 rods three feet north of Totoket path by a large rock marked.*

"I think this is what we've been looking for," Dwight confirmed. "This is Daniel's farm. Let's get a copy of this made and check the Assessor's office down the hall."

The secretary in the Assessor's office was surprised by their request. She told them that old records were stored in the attic and it would take some time to locate them. Dwight left a phone number and said they would return. They obtained a map of Guilford before they left the building. Back in his apartment, Dwight attempted to locate Daniel's farm on the map. To their surprise, it wasn't there. It was further east.

"It must be in Madison," he concluded. "We'll get a map of Madison tomorrow and find it." But an examination of the Madison map indicated that the eighteen acres was still further east and it remained for them to obtain a map of Clinton.

"Wow," Dwight observed. "Here it is. It's almost in the center of Clinton, just north of Route 1. And the Amtrak run right through the northeast part of the property."

"What's our next move?" Karen asked.

"I need some legal help," he told her. "The next step is beyond me."

*

Roger Rowland regarded the New Haven Green from the window of his law office on the seventh floor and thought about retirement. At seventy-five he looked back on many years of a successful law practice and a happy marriage. A distinguished looking man, still robust, with piercing gray eyes, a ready smile and hair graying at the temples. His musings were interrupted by the buzz of his intercom.

"There's a Mr. Morrow here to see you," his secretary announced. "He says he has an appointment with you but I don't..."

"Yes, he called me at home. Please send him in." He remembered the phone call very well because of its unusual nature. Dwight entered the office, shook Roger's proffered hand and sat down.

"Mr. Rowland, as I told you the other night, I'm a second year law student at Yale. My girl friend became interested in this bizarre situation that appears to involve one of your ancestors."

"One of *my* ancestors? Please go on."

"Yes," Dwight continued, "his name is Daniel Rowland and we have compelling reasons to believe that he is your great, great, great grandfather."

"You have used the present tense, young man. You mean "was."

"No sir," Dwight told him. "He's alive."

"Now surely that's not possible. That would make the man something over...perhaps two hundred years old. As a law student you must learn to deal strictly with facts and not..."

"Please let me present the evidence, sir." Roger leaned back in his chair.

"Very well, go ahead. I might as well hear the whole story. In for a penny, in for a pound as the English say."

Dwight related the incident as described by Daniel. He told how Joseph found him on the beach, of Daniel's familiarity with colonial Guilford, the coins, the results of the medical and dental examinations, his familiarity with an obscure colonial author, and Daniel's actions during the bank robbery. Roger listened with mounting interest. He shook his head in disbelief.

"I can't believe it. It's just not possible. This sounds like some kind of a hoax. Couldn't he have researched all this information?"

"Yes, but for what purpose? He lived with Professor Pellegrini for over a year before he moved out. There's no record of him in any of the government agencies. Until he became ill he was happy working as a farmer. If this is a scam it must be the most elaborate one I've ever heard of with no apparent goal. I know it defies all scientific explanations but here he is. I had...still have, difficulty believing it myself. But I must tell you sir, I do believe he's genuine. And his knowledge of colonial Guilford is remarkable. Details that are buried in old books and papers." Roger was silent for a moment.

"But my family comes from Cleveland."

"Actually, we were able to trace your family back to New Haven and Guilford," Dwight told him.

"Well, a DNA test should be able to reveal if there is a family connection. How old is this man?"

"I believe he's thirty-seven, sir."

"What would you want me to do?"

"Sir, he had a farm. The farm was granted to his father for military service. The land is in Clinton and the Amtrak goes across it. A police firing range and a town dump may be on it. As far as I have been able to determine, his descendents, and that includes you, have never been compensated for that land. He would like the land returned to his family."

"How about taxes? Maybe his farm was seized for being in arrears."

"I don't know that. We're checking with the Assessor's Office in Guilford."

"Where is he now?"

"He's living with a college professor in Hamden. He's recuperating from a wound he received foiling a bank robbery." Dwight told him about the attempted holdup. Roger rose and shook hands with Dwight.

"I tell you what. I'll pay him a visit. Leave your phone number with my secretary. If I decide to take this case, we'll work together. But we'll surely be laughed out of court."

After Dwight left, Roger ruminated about the strange case. He thought of his father, growing up, college, his service in the Navy, law school, his marriage, his sons. Family, that's what is important. If this Daniel is really related to me...to us, then he surely deserves my help. But a 36-year old great-great-great grandfather. That's bizarre.

CHAPTER 19

Dwight and Karen visited Daniel a week later. Dwight described his meeting with Roger. He explained the DNA test to Daniel and asked for his permission to have the test done.

"Of a certainty," Daniel told him. "If Roger is indeed my kinsman then I presume that this test will prove it. After all, blood is thicker than water." Dwight smiled.

"I have some good news. I've found definite proof of the location and legality of your farm. By the way, Daniel, did you pay taxes?"

"Indeed. Every man between sixteen and sixty years of age paid a poll tax each year."

"I meant taxes on your land."

"That too. Each acre of meadow was taxed one dollar and a half; planted land, a dollar and sixty-seven cents; pasture was one dollar and thirty cents and woods were thirty-four cents the acre. Each cow and mare were taxed twelve pence. We had little money so we paid in corn or wheat and sometimes partly in flax."

"Thanks, Daniel. That's very helpful. I'll keep working on it."

*

Roger opened the envelope containing the results of the DNA tests. The report explained, "DNA analysis of STR and Y chromosomes performed on samples obtained from Daniel Rowland and from yourself, reveal the same Y chromosome haplotype. These results do not prove or disprove that Daniel Rowland is your great-great-great grandfather. No test can determine that relationship. These results do provide strong evidence that you and he are closely related."

Roger was astounded. He thought about Daniel ever since Dwight's visit and he came to the conclusion that it was some kind of a hoax. But now, this report. He decided to visit Daniel. He drove to the Pellegrini home in Hamden and introduced himself to Linda.

She took Roger upstairs to Daniel's room. Daniel was asleep and for a time Roger stood quietly at the bedside and studied his features. He was startled by Daniel's resemblance to his own sons. Daniel became aware of his visitor and opened his eyes. They were gray like Roger's eyes and those of his sons. Roger extended his hand.

"My name is Roger Rowland. I understand we're family." Daniel sat up and shook his hand.

"I am very pleased to make your acquaintance. Pray, sit down." There was an awkward silence for a few moments.

"I'm an attorney," Roger started, "and I'd like to help you...our family. Could you tell me as much as you can about yourself, from the very beginning?" Daniel nodded.

"I was born in Guilford on the tenth of March, seventeen and fifty-three. I lived on our farm with my parents. My mother died when I was seven. I had little schooling save a few months at our school at Flag Marsh. I worked on our farm with my father. He died in 1779 leaving me the farm and a small amount of money, twelve pounds and eight shillings. I married Elizabeth Hubbard in 1785; we had a little girl but alas, the child died of the croup after only one year of life..."

Roger listened carefully. He had learned to distinguish veracity from falsehood after many years of listening to his client's accounts, many of which were fabrications. Daniel's narrative had the ring of truth.

"Tell me about the war, Daniel; the Revolution. Was there fighting in Guilford?"

"Well, it started in 1775. Most of the folk in Guilford were patriotic; even those loyal to King George felt that those new taxes were unfair. There was little fighting in Connecticut; it was mostly raids. We built a guardhouse on the shore and in May of seventy-nine Colonel Meigs and a group of Connecticut men sailed over and raided the British at Sag Harbor on Long

Island and burned their barracks. Nigh on a month later some British and Tories crossed the Sound and attacked us. They landed at Sachem's Head, burned Simeon Leete's house and the guardhouse and marched up to the village. Captain Peter Vail and our Guilford Company were ready for them. They fired on the Redcoats and drove them back to their boats. Two of our Guilford men, Simeon Leete and Ebenezer Hart, were killed."

"Were you in any of these battles?"

"Nay, Roger. I took my turn in the watch at the guardhouse. I was on my farm when the fighting occurred."

"How did you come to be here, Daniel?"

Daniel related the happening with the dark cloud, waking up in the hospital and going to live with Joseph Pellegrini and his family.

"And what have you been doing since?"

"Ah, I found work on a farm nearby until I was wounded."

"I heard that you were involved in thwarting a bank robbery."

"Indeed! Those scoundrels shot an unarmed man and kept the rest of us in the bank in terror. There was a babe in its mother's arms who cried from hunger. I did what I could to be of help and alas, was shot for my pains."

"How can I be of help to you, Daniel?"

"Well, my farm is gone. The land was given to my father by the Guilford town fathers and should remain in our family. I would fain learn what became of it and mayhap get it back." Roger nodded.

"I'm not promising anything but I'll do what I can. It was a pleasure meeting you, Daniel." He stood up to leave, then turned back. "It seems...bizarre that you, a young man, are apparently my great-great-great grandfather. I have difficulty believing that."

"I, too. I can accept that we are kin, but to have a great-great-great grandson of your years addles my mind."

They both laughed.

*

Several weeks later Dwight met with Roger to report his findings. He explained that as colonial Guilford had expanded eastward, new communities like Madison and Clinton developed and eventually became towns. Over the years the Rowland Farm that was initially in Guilford, came to be in Madison and eventually in present day Clinton.

"It also appears that Clinton has put a Police range and a town dump on the property."

"What about taxes?" Roger asked.

"As far as I can determine, taxes were paid to Madison until the property was condemned around 1850."

"Was any payment made for the property?"

"I could find no deed or record of transfer or payment."

"Let's get started then," Roger said. "The first step is to send letters to the defendants with our claims and demands for remedy. We will demand that the railroad remove their tracks from Daniel's land and pay for past usage; and we will ask the Town of Clinton to remove the range and dump from the property and compensate Daniel for the years of use."

"Find out all you can about the railroads that crossed Daniel's property," Roger continued. "We also need to know when the property was in Madison and when it became a part of Clinton. Also, are there any court records of Decrees Quieting Title or other title changes? We will have a big problem with the statute of limitations. Somehow we have to find a way around that. You might want to bone up on Real Estate Law."

"I'll get right on it."

I don't believe I'm really doing this, Roger thought, but somehow I know that Daniel's story is true.

CHAPTER 20

Since the day, many months ago, when he learned that Joseph was Roman Catholic, Daniel had not broached the subject of going to church. Yet every Sunday he felt guilty for not attending divine services as he and Elizabeth were accustomed. He mentioned it to Betsy.

"I'd be glad to take you, Daniel, but I'm Anglican. That's Church of England and I don't think you'd be comfortable there." Joseph solved the problem.

"Your Puritan church in Guilford became the First Congregational Church. I've spoken to Roger about this. He attends the Congregational Church in New Haven and he said he'd be delighted to have you join him for services this Sunday."

Roger picked Daniel up on the following Sunday morning and together they drove to New Haven.

"Where is the meeting house?" Daniel asked.

"The church is right there on the Green." Roger pointed out a white building with a steeple.

"Why do you call it a meeting house?"

"Well, our building was used for prayer and for town meetings," Daniel explained. "Truly, the church is the people." The organ was playing as they entered the church and took seats near to the front.

"Methinks you must pay a goodly amount of taxes for so fair a pew," Daniel remarked.

"What do you mean?"

"Is this not your seat?"

"No, you can sit anywhere you want. Were seats assigned in your meeting house?"

"Of a certainty. They were assigned each year by the church elders according to the tax rolls. Special seats were saved for dignified persons." Daniel observed the stained glass windows, the cross in front of the pulpit, and the choir dressed in burgundy robes with white collars.

Two ministers, wearing white robes and multicolored stoles, entered and took seats on the raised choir loft in the front. Daniel was amazed to see that one of them was a woman. After all the worshippers had found their seats, the woman minister rose, welcomed everyone and invited them to greet the people seated nearby. Roger stood and shook hands with his neighbors and Daniel followed his example. The minister announced the opening hymn that everyone seemed to know. She read a prayer of invocation and the service continued with a lesson from the scripture. This was followed by the Offering. Roger and Daniel each placed a dollar in the plate. There were several more hymns, some sung by the choir. The woman minister sat down, and the other minister read a scriptural lesson and then delivered a short sermon. The sermon was entitled "In my Father's house are many mansions," and dealt with respecting other religions. After another hymn, he pronounced a benediction and, to Daniel's surprise, the service ended. The service had lasted about an hour and a half. The organ played as the people filed out of the church. Both ministers stood just outside of the doorway shaking hands with the people as they left. Roger shook hands with one of the ministers and introduced Daniel.

"Reverend Hutchison, I'd like you to meet my...cousin, Daniel Rowland." Reverend Michael Hutchison was a tall man in his fifties, with piercing blue eyes, gray hair and an athletic frame.

"Always glad to see another Rowland." He turned to Daniel and shook his hand vigorously.

"Where are you from?"

"He's from Guilford," Roger answered before Daniel could respond.

"How did our service compare with the one you are accustomed to in Guilford?" the minister asked.

"Well sir, I would not wish to commit an indecorum on the Sabbath but I presume that by some misunderstanding my kinsman and I have just attended a Romish or Papist service.

Now truly, it was in no way offensive to me but..." The minister's mouth dropped open.

"What!" he exclaimed. "I don't believe what I'm hearing." He turned to Roger, expecting an explanation. Roger sighed.

"Perhaps we could have a little talk." They followed the minister to his office in a small building at the rear of the church. He removed his robe, waved them to comfortable chairs and offered them coffee.

"I hardly know how to begin," Roger said. "It's so unbelievable." He went on to relate the story. Daniel sat in silence, occasionally drumming his fingers on his thigh.

"Oh yes, I read about him...you. You're the young man who foiled that bank robbery in Hamden." Daniel nodded assent. The minister sat back in his chair and regarded him quietly.

"Did all this *really* happen? Perhaps you imagined it...a bad dream, some illness, I mean how is it possible? You would be more than two hundred years old!"

"I would to Heaven it *were* all a bad dream and I was back with my Elizabeth," Daniel exclaimed, "but here I remain."

"Roger, do you believe this?"

"There is some very convincing evidence that Daniel is telling the truth even though there is no scientific explanation. Yes, I believe it." The minister shook his head slowly. He turned to Daniel.

"You said that you found today's service strange. How was it different from the ones you used to hear?"

"Everything was different. Church was very stern. The meeting house was very plain; there were no ornaments, no music. There was no heat in the winter. The services lasted all day. We were fined if we failed to attend. The pastor wore a plain, black gown with a white collar. Of a certainty there were no women ministers..."

"Please go on," the minister prompted.

"There was no collection...Offering. We paid a tax to the church once a year. And I saw some Christmas hymns in your hymn book. We did not celebrate Christmas." The minister nodded.

"Yes, I know about that. The English had a custom of giving presents to their servants and sometimes even changing places with them on the day after Christmas. It was called St. Stephen's Day or Boxing Day and at times Christmas was associated with considerable drunkenness and debauchery. The Puritans wanted no part of that." Daniel nodded and continued.

"There were no books, for many of us could not read. We knew no hymns. We sang psalms but forsooth each sang to his own tune. The sermons were very long indeed...mayhap, two hours or more and verily of a different slant."

"How different?"

"Well sir, we were Puritans. Our pastor taught that we...that man was corrupt by Adam's sin and totally depraved but that some were selected by God for salvation. That we must turn away from sin and have faith in Jesus Christ. And that those who did not believe should get out; they would be damned."

"That's all Old New England theology, Daniel," the minister explained. "The Congregational Church has changed considerably over the last two hundred years. We have become more optimistic, more liberal. As you have seen, women are now ordained as ministers. We are more ecumenical."

"That word is strange to me," Daniel said, "and I do not know its meaning."

"It means that we have become more tolerant. That we recognize and respect other religions. We don't believe that God requires a uniformity of religions."

"Do we still send missionaries to the heathens, the Indians and to China and India?"

"Yes, there are still missionaries but they no longer attempt to convert others to Christianity. We now preach faith in God, fellowship in the church and freedom of worship and conscience."

"Also," Roger added, "one of the first things that happened was the requirement that churches remove from public land.

This was because of increasing belief in the separation of church and state. Back around 1670, Roger Williams, the founder of Rhode Island, put forth that idea and almost a hundred years later Thomas Jefferson strongly advocated the separation of church and state. It became the law of the land with the First Amendment to the Constitution."

*

On his final post-operative visit to the hospital, the doctor informed Daniel about the consequences of his wound.

"As you know, Mr. Rowland, we were forced to remove one of your kidneys and your spleen because of the extreme damage to those organs caused by the bullet. Now you can live with one kidney without any problems but I must warn you that the loss of your spleen makes you susceptible to severe infections by certain bacteria."

"I do not discover your meaning, doctor," Daniel told him. "What must I do?"

"You must be very careful. What appears to be a slight illness may rapidly become fatal for you. I will give you some capsules of an antibiotic and a prescription for more. You should start taking this medicine at the first sign of a fever and see a doctor immediately. Even just a cold."

"Forsooth sir, I am not disposed to seek out doctors."

"Please believe me, Mr. Rowland. It could save your life."

*

Linda answered the phone.

"It's for you, Daniel," she said.

"Of a certainty?"

"You're the only Daniel Rowland here." she laughed and handed him the phone. This was Daniel's first actual experience talking on the phone.

"Just speak in here naturally," she instructed.

"Ah,...hello?"

"Mr. Rowland? Daniel Rowland?"

"Yes."

"Mr. Rowland, my name is Don Westmorland. I'm the chairman of the Republican Party here in Hamden. We read about your actions in stopping that bank robbery a few months ago. We need men like you in our party. May I ask if you are a registered Republican?"

"Nay sir, I am not registered with any party."

"That's O.K. Would you be willing to get together with a few of us? We will be meeting Tuesday evening at seven in Morgan's Restaurant. It's right across from the A & P."

"Truly good sir, I would be pleased to meet with you."

"Great! See you Tuesday night."

*

Morgan's was a small bar and restaurant on a main street. Linda and Daniel were shown into a small room in the rear. Four men and a woman were seated at a table. The men rose and one of them introduced himself.

"Hi, Mr. Rowland. I'm Don Westmorland. We spoke on the phone the other night." He introduced the others.

"Is this Mrs. Rowland?"

"I'm Linda Pellegrino, a friend." Westmorland extended his hand.

"Please sit down. Can we get you anything to drink? Can we call you Daniel?"

"That is my name."

"Daniel, you told me that you are not registered with any political party. How do you feel about some of the issues that we Republicans favor?"

"Why sir, for the soul of me I do not discover what they may be. I am a simple farmer " Westmorland smiled.

"The Republican platform is for individual rights, family values, education and child care. We also favor open markets for agricultural products and a strong anti-crime bill."

"Indeed sir, those are all fine things," Daniel said. "I deem those markets the best place to buy food and garments. I am astonished at how fast those clerks can take your money." The men and the woman glanced at each other.

"Ah yes," Westmorland continued. "May I ask you what is your position on the abortion issue?" Daniel was embarrassed.

"It is surely a grievous sin."

"Daniel, have you ever considered running for public office?"

"Nay, sir. Surely you jest. I have little schooling save reading, writing and ciphering." The group became more bewildered and confused with Daniel's ambiguous responses. After fifteen minutes Westmorland rose.

"Well, thank you, Daniel, for taking the time to come down and talk with us. It was a pleasure to meet you."

As they drove home, Daniel commented, "Indeed, the Republicans propose to do only good things. What do their enemies say?" Linda laughed.

"I wouldn't exactly call the Democrats their enemies, but they do see things differently from the Republicans. The Democrats propose economic growth, improving education, protecting the environment, improving health care, fighting crime and, let's see, welfare reform."

"Those all sound like good things, too. In what manner do those parties differ?"

"Well, they differ in their basic philosophy. The Republicans believe that most problems should be left to state and local governments to solve. They tend to favor industry and business. The Democrats expect the Federal government to deal with many social problems and they tend to support labor, you know, unions. There are also differences about some basic issues like prayer in public schools, affirmative action, abortion and gun control."

"I do not understand. What has the government to do with guns and prayers in school and those other things?"

"It's complicated," Linda explained. "Many Democrats want to make people get licenses for guns, especially handguns, because many crimes and murders are committed with them. Their opponents claim that the Constitution guarantees the right of people to have guns."

"A man should be able to have a musket or a rifle and a fowling piece for hunting. That is only right," Daniel declared.

"Yes, but some people want to have automatic weapons, you know, assault rifles, machine guns..."

"Ah, those are terrible things. Why would any man want to possess them? And, pray explain about the prayers in school? Our schoolmaster always began the lessons each day by reading from the bible. For the soul of me I cannot see the harm in that."

"Well, some folks feel that it violates the separation of church and state specified in the Constitution." They rode in silence for a few minutes.

Then Daniel asked diffidently, "Pray explain that matter...about abortion?"

"Joe and I are Catholics and our religion forbids abortion but we, and many other people, strongly believe that only the woman should have the right to decide what is done with her body. And the Supreme Court has upheld that principle but many people strongly oppose it."

"Of a certainty," Daniel told her as she pulled into the driveway, "politics has become very complicated."

CHAPTER 21

"Well counselor, what were you able to find out?" Roger asked. Dwight grinned at the use of the title.

"Actually, Karen and I found quite a bit. The land was granted to Daniel's father, Isaac, in 1759 and passed to Daniel twenty years later. Daniel's wife died in 1828 and no one lived on the property, but taxes continued to be paid by Daniel's son, Noah. New boundaries were established in 1834 and the land became part of the Town of Madison. Five years later there was another boundary change and the property became part of the Town of Clinton. Then, in 1848, this guy, Simon Mumford, moved on to the property and claimed the land by adverse possession."

"How long did he live there?" Roger asked.

"Is that important?"

"Yes," Roger explained, "because to claim land by adverse possession the person must actually live on the land continuously for at least five years with the owner's knowledge but without the owner's permission and during those five years the claimant must pay all the taxes."

"Well I don't know whether the Rowland family knew about Mumford," Dwight told him "but he only lived there about three years and paid no taxes. Also, he gave the New Haven and New London Railroad Company permission to lay tracks across the property."

"Mumford's claim was illegal," Roger said. "The property still belonged to the Rowland family. Then what?"

"Nothing seems to have happened until 1945 when the Town of Clinton claimed the land by eminent domain and put a police firing range on the property. And in 1950, they put a town dump there."

"Eminent domain permits a local or federal government to appropriate private land for public use. I believe that claim is fraudulent also. We'll file our complaints with the Superior

Court of Connecticut. The court will then issue a summons and we will serve the summons and the complaints on the Town of Clinton, the railroad and the Transit Authority. We will demand a jury trial and compensatory damages of three million dollars."

"How did you arrive at that figure?"

"The railroad used the land for one hundred and forty-nine years and I charged them a thousand bucks a month. Clinton used the property for fifty-four years with their police range and forty-nine years with the dump. I charged them a thousand a month for each. Then, eighteen acres in downtown Clinton at two hundred and fifty per. What did you learn about the railroad?" Dwight reached into his briefcase and took out more papers.

"The New Haven and New London Railroad Company was chartered in 1848 and began to lay track in 1850 but two years later they went belly up. The General Assembly in Hartford absorbed the defunct company and reorganized it as the New Haven, New London and Stonington Railroad. Then, it was reorganized again in 1864 as the Shore Line and in 1870 the entire property was leased to the New York, New Haven Railroad. Two years later, that became the New York, New Haven and Hartford Railroad which, in 1969, was absorbed into the Penn Central System and later into Amtrak, Metro North and the Connecticut Transit Authority."

Roger smiled. "Those are the guys we're going after."

*

Two weeks later, the phone rang in Roger Rowland's office. His secretary announced, "It's a Sheldon Bush from the Connecticut Transit Authority."

"Put him on. Good morning, Mr. Bush. I've been expecting your call. How can I help you?"

"Mr. Rowland, I represent the Transit Authority. We received your claim letter. You and your client can't be serious about this matter?"

"We are very serious, Mr. Bush. We have had similar responses from the railroad and the defendants in the other suit. We intend to proceed."

"What other suit?"

"We are filing a similar claim against the Town of Clinton."

"But you're dealing with something that may have occurred more than a hundred years ago. Surely the statute of limitations would bar such actions."

"We'll address that at the proper time. Good day, Mr. Bush."

*

They waited in the judge's chambers, Roger, Dwight, and the lawyers representing the defendants. They all rose as Judge Frederick Johnson entered, a tall black man with short gray hair. He motioned them to be seated.

"This hearing is called to order," he said, sitting down behind his desk. "Let's get started. Who all is here?"

Roger stood up. "Roger Rowland, your honor, for the plaintiff, and my colleague Dwight Morrow." He sat down.

"Are you related to the plaintiff?" the judge asked.

"Yes, your honor, I am."

"Let's proceed."

"I'm Sheldon Bush, your honor, representing defendant The Transit Authority."

"Miles Conway, representing defendant Amtrak.

"And I'm Susan Dellasandro, representing defendant the Town of Clinton. The judge addressed the group.

Mr. Rowland, your motion for joinder is sustained."

"Thank you, your honor."

"What's that? Dwight whispered to Roger.

"It permits us to include all the defendants in one lawsuit," Roger explained. Sheldon Bush raised his hand.

"Your honor, this suit should be time-barred since it exceeds the twenty-year statute of limitations by more than a hundred years. I move for dismissal under Rule 12."

"I'm well aware of the length of the statute of limitations, Mr. Bush." The judge turned to Roger.

"Mr. Rowland?" Roger stood up.

"Judge, we acknowledge that the statute of limitations has been exceeded. However, as we shall show, there are some very unusual circumstances in this case. I will also cite a precedent in the California Code dealing with Consumer Law that states the statute of limitations doesn't begin until the defendant has been apprised of the..."

"This is Connecticut, not California, Mr. Rowland. Nevertheless I'll take the motion for dismissal under advisement." Miles Conway got up.

"Judge, it has come to our attention that the plaintiff claims to have been born in 1753. That would make him two hundred and forty-six years old. Since human beings don't live that long, he is not a natural person and according to the Fifth Amendment due process is limited to natural persons." He sat down with a satisfied smile.

"Your honor," Roger responded, "in the equal protection clause of the Fourteenth Amendment, "person" has been held to include natural and artificial persons. Furthermore, our client was born in Connecticut and as such he is a citizen of this state and of the United States and is entitled to due process under the law." The judge smiled.

"Nice try, Mr. Conway."

"Judge," Susan Dellasandro interjected, " I suggest that the matter has already been settled by *laches* in that there has been an undue lapse of time to enforce the right to an action. I would like to move for estoppel by laches." She looked expectantly at the judge. Judge Johnson smiled at her.

"Thank you for the law lesson, Miss Dellasandro. I will take your motion under advisement. Well, gentlemen and madam counselor, this has been most interesting. Let's see what discovery will produce. This hearing is adjourned."

"What happens now?" Dwight asked, as he and Roger left the courthouse.

"We wait for the judge to rule on the motions. If he denies them we enter the discovery phase where each side has the opportunity to learn about the other side's evidence and witnesses that will be presented at trial. They can use interrogatories, which are basically questionnaires sent to the opposing side, and depositions where witnesses are examined. The ball is in their court."

"And if the judge grants either of the motion?" Dwight asked.

"Then that's the end of the ball game."

*

"We've received interrogatories from Clinton and from Amtrak," Roger announced as Dwight entered his office on a Saturday morning. "They seems to anticipate that the judge will deny the motion. They're not even waiting for the ruling."

"What are they asking for?"

"As you might expect," Roger said, "they are asking for the legal basis of our claim. We will start by pointing out that Section 47-1 of the Connecticut General Statutes states that colonial grants are valid and that each property by fee simple has absolute dominion to their kin, successors and assignees forever. That means that the grant is of infinite duration and absolute inheritance, free of any conditions, limitations or restrictions to the heirs."

"I see." Dwight indicated. "Then what?"

"Then, we state that the Simon Mumford claim on the property by adverse possession is invalid since he didn't live there for the five years as required and he paid no taxes."

"That means that Mumford had no right to authorize the railroad to lay track across the property since it wasn't his."

"Right." Roger told him. "It also means that the railroad was trespassing. Then the Town of Clinton condemned the property and laid claim to it by eminent domain. But, the Fifth Amendment to the U.S. Constitution and the Connecticut Statutes as well, both state that for land to be taken by eminent domain, the property must be appraised and the owner,that's the Rowlands, be paid the fair market value of the land. There is no record of any appraisal and no payment was ever made to the Rowland family. It also means," Roger continued, "that the Town of Clinton was also guilty of trespass by constructing the police range and the dump on Rowland land."

"It looks like we're in a very strong position," Dwight offered.

"Our weakest point is the statute of limitations. Under Connecticut civil and criminal law if no legal action is taken within twenty years from the damage or crime, there is no basis for legal action. The one exception is murder; the statute of limitations doesn't apply to murder."

"So what's our position?"

"Well, I cited a California statute that says the statute of limitations doesn't start until the defendant knows about the issue. It's a long shot but the judge said he'd take it under advisement. At this point it's a crap shoot."

CHAPTER 22

STATE OF CONNECTICUT SUPERIOR COURT

Daniel Rowland, Plaintiff vs Amtrak, Connecticut Transport Authority and Town of Clinton, Defendants.

Transcript of examination before trial of Joseph Pellegrini, September 15, 1999

Appearances:

Roger Rowland, Esq. Attorney for Plaintiff
Sheldon Bush, Esq. Attorney for Defendant
Miles Conway, Esq. Attorney for Defendant
Susan Dellasandro, Esq. Attorney for Defendant
Catherine L. Sherr, Court Reporter

JOSEPH PELLEGRINI, being duly sworn, testified as follows:

EXAMINATION BY MR. BUSH:

Q. Professor Pellegrini, my name is Sheldon Bush. I represent the Connecticut Transit Authority. These other lawyers are Miles Conway representing Amtrak and Susan Dellasandro for the Town of Clinton. Have you ever testified at a deposition before?
A. No.
Q. I will be asking you questions. You have to answer "yes" or "no." Shaking your head or answering "hmm" or "uh huh" will only confuse the court reporter. Also, if you don't understand any question, you must tell me. Will you do that?
A. Yes.
Q. Can you state your full name?
A. Joseph Pellegrini.
Q. And where do you reside?

A. 12 Andover Street, Hamden, Connecticut.
Q. What is your occupation?
A. I'm a professor of history at Quinnipiac College.
Q. How long have you been employed there?
A. Nineteen years.
Q. Are you acquainted with Daniel Rowland?
A. Yes.
Q. How long have you known Mr. Rowland?
A. About two years.
Q. How did you meet him?
A. We found him unconscious on the beach in Guilford.
Q. Can you describe the circumstances?
A. Well, my wife and I and our two children were walking along the Westwood Trail leading to the beach. We were planning to picnic there. Our kids ran ahead and discovered him.
Q. Mr. Rowland?
A. Yes. He was unconscious and dressed in what appeared to be a colonial costume.
Q. What happened then?
A. My wife ran back to the car and used the cell phone to call for help. The paramedics came in an ambulance and took him to the hospital. I went with them.
Q. Why did you go along with them?
A. I was curious. Also, it didn't seem right to, you know, abandon an unknown person.
Q. What happened in the hospital?
A. Well, they treated him and he regained consciousness. He seemed totally unfamiliar with everyday things, like bathrooms, electric lights, cars, telephones, things like that. And his language was archaic.
Q. Did he speak English?
A. Yes, but it sounded like the English spoken in colonial times.
Q. How would you know that, professor?
A. That is my area of expertise; the American Colonial Period.
Q. I see. Then what happened?

A. Well, Linda...my wife, came and we brought him home to Hamden. He lived with us for over a year.
Q. Professor Pellegrini, did Mr. Rowland ever explain how he came to be on the beach in Guilford?
A. Yes.
Q. Could you tell us about that?
A. Well, he left his farm to go to the marsh to dig some clams and...
Q. When was that?
A. He told us it was August 9th.
Q. What year?
A. Seventeen ninety.
Q. Seventeen ninety! And when did you find him?
A. June 12th, 1998.
Q. That's two hundred and...eight years. Where did he say he had been all that time?
A. He doesn't know.
Q. I see. And how did he get here?
A. He...we don't know. Some strange kind of storm cloud.
Q. How can you explain that?
A. I can't.
Q. Professor Pellegrini, you're an educated man. You have a Ph.D., you teach at a college. Doesn't a tale about someone riding on a cloud from 1790 strain your credulity?
A. It's very difficult to believe and there's no scientific explanation but the evidence...
Q. What evidence is that?
A. Well, he had two coins with him from that period, his clothing was all hand made, he never had any shots or dental work, there was no record of him in any government agency, he was familiar with little-known details of colonial Guilford and an author of that period. There are records of his father, his wife and his son...
Q. Wouldn't it be possible for a person to research all that information?
A. I guess so, but why...?

Q. Thank you, professor. I have no further questions.

EXAMINATION BY MR. CONWAY:

Q. Professor, to your knowledge, has Mr. Rowland ever been examined by a psychiatrist?
A. Yes.
Q. When was that?
A. The dean brought in a psychiatrist to examine Mr. Rowland.
Q. Do you know the results of that examination?
A. No.
Q. Thank you. No further questions.

EXAMINATION BY MS. DELLASANDRO:

Q. Professor Pellegrini, don't you think that it is quite a coincidence that the one person who found and sheltered a visitor from colonial days just happens to be a professor of American Colonial History?

MR. ROWLAND Objection. Leading the witness. You may answer the question.

A. Yes, I guess so.
Q. Thank you. No further questions.
(Whereupon the Examination concluded).

*

"How was the deposition?" Linda asked when Joseph returned from Hartford.

"There were three lawyers and each one made me out as very gullible and Daniel as either a nut or a crook."

The phone rang. Joseph picked it up. "Hello."

"Professor Pellegrini, this is Bob Hunt from the *Register*."

"I have nothing to say to you, Mr. Hunt. Good bye!"

"Please don't hang up," the reporter blurted, "I think I may be able to help Daniel Rowland."

"How could you do that?"

"I could write a story describing Daniel's efforts to regain his land. That might influence the judge and the jury. Don't under estimate the power of the press." Joseph regarded this offer with suspicion.

"Why would you want to do that?"

"Well, I think he's a right guy. The way he behaved in that bank robbery. I'd like to help."

"How did you learn about...the legal stuff?" Joseph asked him.

"I cover the courts," the reporter explained, "and I saw his name on the calendar so I checked. It's my job."

"Go see Roger Rowland. He's an attorney in New Haven. If he'll go along with the idea, he can give you all the details."

*

The story appeared a week later in *The New Haven Register*.

HAMDEN HERO SEEKS RETURN OF HIS LAND

By Tom Hunt

HAMDEN, CT. Daniel Rowland, 35, who months ago was instrumental in foiling the attempted robbery of a bank in Hamden and causing the surrender of the two robbers is now seeking justice in the court. Mr. Rowland, who was seriously wounded in the robbery, is hoping to regain the land that was his family's farm. The property was granted to Mr. Rowland's father for military service by the Guilford town administration but the land is now in Clinton, as a result of boundary changes. Amtrak has laid tracks across the property and the Town of Clinton put a police firing range and a

> dump on the property, all apparently without asking permission of the Rowland family. Mr. Rowland's attorney, Roger Rowland, a distant relative, says that a major problem in the case is the statute of limitations, the lapse of time before legal action was started, but he is hopeful that an exception can be found.

*

"Karen and I have finished digging in the records and now we think we know what happened to your farm." Dwight said. They were sitting in Roger's office while Roger was in court.

"Pray tell me, friend Dwight."

"After Elizabeth died in 1828, your son Noah continued to pay the taxes and the land just lay there until 1834 when the State of Connecticut changed some boundaries and your farm, that had been in Guilford became part of the Town of Madison. The State changed things again and your land now is part of the Town of Clinton. Then this man, Simon Mumford, moved on to your land and claimed it as his."

"The scoundrel! A squatter. Could he do that?"

"He could," Dwight explained, "if he lived on the land for five years without your family's permission, and if he paid all the taxes. But, he was only there for three years or so and he didn't pay any taxes, so his claim is invalid. Also. Mumford gave the railroad permission to lay tracks across the land."

"Oho! I dare not ask. What happened next?"

"Nothing much happened for almost a hundred years but then in 1945 the Town of Clinton claimed the land and put a police firing range and a dump on it."

"Upon my word! How could they do that?"

"There's a law that says if the town needs a piece of private land they can condemn it and take it over, but, and this is important, the town must evaluate the land and pay the owner a fair price. They never did that." Daniel was angry.

"Is there any chance that my farm can be recovered?"

"We're going to try our best, Daniel. The problem is that all these things happened so long ago. Would you settle for some payment for the land?"

"Nay! That is Rowland land, given to my father and farmed by Elizabeth and me. Our little daughter lies buried somewhere on it. I would fain have the land back."

"What would you do with the land? It's practically in downtown Clinton, not far from a housing development."

"Methinks I would give it to my kinsman, Roger, since it rightfully belongs to him and his children. Roger could build him a house there. Mayhap I could live there and farm it."

CHAPTER 23

Art Woodward became very excited when he read Hunt's story about Daniel in *The New Haven Register*. He was the producer of *Extraordinary Folks*, a TV program. He lost no time in calling Leslie Graham, the show's host.

"Leslie, I've got a good one for the show. How about a guy who says he was born in 1753, is suing the Town of Clinton, the railroad and the State of Connecticut to get his farm back and got shot stopping a bank robbery in Hamden?"

"He sounds terrific!" she told him. "Try to get him. Call him up."

Extraordinary Folks, a popular human interest show ran Sunday mornings on WTEH, a CBS affiliate in New Haven. The show featured Leslie Graham, an attractive, animated woman who interviewed one or more guests each week; people who had unusual life experiences to relate.

Daniel's reaction to Art's phone call was a mixture of surprise and bewilderment.

"Bless me, sir! I am astonished...I am not disposed to...I do not discover...Pray, speak to my friend Joe."

Art explained to Joseph that they would like to have Daniel on the show. He pointed out that the publicity might help Daniel's legal efforts. Joseph consulted with Roger who felt Daniel's appearance on the show would not affect the case. It was much later that Roger realized how wrong he was. Linda and Betsy encouraged Daniel to accept the invitation. Nick and Cathy were enthusiastic in urging him to be on the show.

"Do it, Daniel! Do it. It'll be great. You'll be on TV."

*

Daniel arrived at the TV station in downtown New Haven. He refused requests to appear in rented colonial garb; he wore a white shirt, open at the neck with no tie and a pair of slacks. His hair was still shoulder length and tied in a queue. Leslie Graham introduced herself.

"How do you do, Daniel. We're very pleased to have you on the show. We will be taping the show and it will appear in a few weeks."

A woman applied make-up to Daniel's face. Leslie showed the cameras to Daniel as they sat down in the set. He was very nervous and he drummed his fingers on his thigh. She tried to put him at ease.

"I'll introduce you to the 'audience,' she explained as a technician attached a small microphone to his shirt. "Then, I'll ask you some questions. Please call me Leslie. Try to forget about the cameras. They'll be moving around all the time. You can look at them or at me."

They started with Leslie announcing, "Good morning. I'm Leslie Graham. Our guest today is Mr. Daniel Rowland. His story is so astounding that it is hard to believe but we have good reasons to think it is true. Good morning, Mr. Rowland."

"Good morning...Leslie." She smiled at him, encouraging.

"What is your occupation, Mr. Rowland?"

"I am a farmer."

"Where is your farm?"

"Ah alas! My farm was in Guilford but it is no longer mine."

"What happened to it?"

"It was taken from my poor wife, Elizabeth and my family by a squatter and...by other towns."

"How did you get your farm?"

"The land was given to my father by the elders of Guilford for his service in the war."

"Which war was that, Mr. Rowland?"

"That was King George's War against the French."

"What year was that?"

"It was in seventeen hundred and fifty-nine."

"Your father lived in 1759?"

"Of a certainty."

"Mr. Rowland, may I ask your age and what year *you* were born?"

"I am thirty-seven years old. I was born in 1753."

"That's amazing. That was 243 years ago. How did you come to be here in 1999?"

"For the soul of me, friend Leslie, I do not know. It is a mystery. I was digging clams on the beach of Leete's Island. There was a sudden storm...this strange cloud..." Daniel described what happened in detail. "And the next thing I knew I was in the Yale Hospital with Joe."

"Joe? Would that be Professor Joseph Pellegrini?"

"Verily." Daniel went on to describe his life with Joseph, Linda and the children. He told of his dear friend, Betsy, living with Mrs. Driscoll and working on Harmon Platt's farm.

"Can you tell us about the bank robbery?"

"Ah forsooth, that was truly an adventure. I had a fancy to place my money in the bank when those two knaves came galloping in with pistols drawn, shouting and frightening us all and demanding money. They shot the guard, a man no longer young and unarmed"

"What did *you* do?"

"Truly, I did nothing until that woman's baby was crying for milk for nigh on to three hours. May I be hanged, I said to myself, if I do not find some milk for that child so I went out to fetch some."

"The robbers let you go?"

"Nay, they threatened to shoot me but I paid them no heed."

"Were you able to get some milk?"

"Aye, and I brought back water and bandages for the wounded man. When one of the robbers began to abuse me I was forced to knock him down. That is when the other one shot me and then pleaded for his life when he could shoot no more. But I could not shoot him." Leslie and the camera crew listened to Daniel's story with rapt attention.

"How did you lose your farm, Mr. Rowland?"

Daniel repeated the events as Dwight had explained them to him. He described the boundary changes that occurred over the years and the squatter, Simon Mumford.

"and then the Town of Clinton took my land for a police range and a dump."

"What would you do if you got the land back?"

"Indeed, I would fain farm it and give it to my kinsman Roger. It is Rowland land."

Leslie turned to the camera crew. "That's a wrap." The big lights were turned off and the crew applauded. She turned to the producer.

"Art, see if you can find someone who we can interview on time travel. Maybe one of the professors from UConn."

*

Professor Malcolm Bainbridge, an English physicist from the University of Connecticut, was delighted with Art's phone call inviting him to appear on the show. His area of specialization was quantum physics and he loved to speculate about some of the arcane aspects of his field. He jumped at the opportunity of being interviewed by Leslie Graham. On camera, in response to Leslie's questions, Bainbridge spoke about the possibility of time travel.

Leslie started, "Professor Bainbridge, stories like *A Connecticut Yankee in King Arthur's Court* by Mark Twain, and H.G. Well's *The Time Machine*, have told of people who were transported from their own time to the past or the future. Is time travel actually possible?"

"There's nothing in the laws of physics or Einstein's rules to prevent time-travel," he told Leslie. He went on to explain concepts like hyperspace, black holes, singularities, worm holes and time warps.

"But didn't your colleague, Steven Hawking from Cambridge, clearly rule out the possibility of time-travel?" she asked. Leslie had done some reading.

"An Israeli scientist found a flaw in Hawking's argument," Bainbridge said. "Of course, there's the time-travel paradox."

"Could you explain that, professor?"

"Well, if you traveled back in time and murdered your own grandmother when she was young, one of your parents wouldn't have been born and therefor you couldn't exist."

"Does that rule out time-travel?" she asked.

"No, they figured out an answer to that problem. It has to do with parallel universes..."

At the end of the interview, Leslie asked him, "Professor Bainbridge, what's your professional opinion about time-travel?"

"We don't know how to do it," he told her, "but I believe it's possible."

*

The show was aired two weeks later and included the interviews with Daniel and Professor Bainbridge. The response was surprising and overwhelming. Letters poured into the station, the vast majority of which expressed belief in Daniel's arrival in this time and sympathy for the loss of his farm. CBS and other national and international news services picked up the story. In China, a news story claimed that the United States discriminated against their own citizens from a former time. Some Russian scientists questioned whether the United States had a secret project researching time travel. The University of Connecticut issued a statement that Professor Bainbridge's opinions did not reflect those of the University. Connecticut senators began receiving phone calls and letters from their constituents demanding fair treatment for Daniel. In Hartford, representatives from Guilford, Madison and Clinton hotly debated the subject of Daniel's farm and in Washington, a Connecticut congressman rose to assure the Congress that "Daniel Rowland is a citizen of our state as long as he lives." Amtrak and the Connecticut Transit Authority received angry letters demanding that their tracks be removed from Daniel's property and a few demonstrators paraded in front of the Connecticut state capitol carrying placards the read "Give Daniel back his farm!" and "Justice for Daniel!"

Joseph had a phone call from Dean Stone.

"You know, Joseph, perhaps we were being somewhat premature in our assessment of Mr. Rowland. All this remarkable publicity should somehow reflect favorably on Quinnipiac. Perhaps he could be a resource for the History Department."

The Pellegrini home was once again besieged by the press, all seeking to interview Daniel, Joseph, Linda or the children. Joseph had to request assistance from the Hamden police to protect the privacy of their house and grounds. Daniel was overwhelmed. He watched himself on TV and listened to the news stories. At first he was excited, then confused and depressed.

What does it all mean? he wondered. He had a slight cold, felt feverish and chilly and went to bed early. Linda found him in bed the next morning after he failed to appear for breakfast. He had a high fever and mumbled incoherently about pills to save his life. She was unable to rouse him and Joseph called an ambulance. Once more Daniel was speeding to the Yale-New Haven Hospital.

CHAPTER 24

By the time Daniel was carried into the Emergency Room he was in a coma and in shock. His skin was cold and clammy, his pulse faint and rapid and his blood pressure was dangerously low. His records revealed that he was asplenic and he was started on intravenous antibiotics and drugs to maintain his blood pressure. An arterial catheter was placed in his neck and he was given oxygen. Bacteria were circulating in his blood. The hospital listed his condition as critical.

Daniel regained consciousness the next day to find Betsy at his bedside. He was unable to speak but he smiled at her. He improved over the next few days and the hospital changed their estimate of his condition to guarded. In fact, he *was* guarded; a police officer was stationed at the door of his room to ensure that only the few authorized visitors were permitted to see him.

By the end of the week the oxygen mask was removed. Daniel was much improved but very weak. Roger hired a private guard to replace the police officer. A few days later the guard came in to ask whether Daniel would see a minister who wished to visit. It was Reverend Michael Hutchison.

"How are you feeling today, Daniel?" he asked.

"I am greatly improved," Daniel told him.

"Is there anything I can do for you?" the minister asked.

"Nay, thank you sir, I am well cared for."

"If you have no objection, I would like to bless you."

"That would be welcome," Daniel told him. The minister gently placed his hand on Daniel's head. Daniel closed his eyes.

"May the Lord bless you and keep you. May the Lord look upon you and be gracious to you. May the Lord turn his face to you and grant you peace. Amen." Daniel opened his eyes and smiled at the minister.

"Would you like to say a prayer?" Reverend Hutchison asked. Daniel nodded. Together they slowly repeated "Our

Father, which art in heaven..." At the end, the minister asked, "Would you like to say a personal prayer?"

Daniel nodded. He thought for a moment and said in a voice that was almost a whisper, "Dear God, I thank thee for all of my friends here, Joe and Linda and their children, my Betsy, Harmon Platt, Mrs. Driscoll, Roger, Dwight and Karen. Bless them and let them be in Thy keeping..." He paused. "And, if it be thy will, may I somehow return to my own time. Amen."

Reverend Hutchison wondered at the simple eloquence of this Connecticut farmer.

"Amen," he repeated.

*

Flowers for Daniel continued to arrive until there was no longer space for them in his room. He asked the nurses to give them to other patients. Some were from Joseph and Linda, Roger, and Karen but many were from unknown well wishers, with messages of encouragement.

Dwight came bursting with news.

"Daniel, your appearance on the TV show with Leslie Graham has really caused a tremendous reaction. Letters are pouring in to the TV station and to state representatives and to the railroad. It was on the national news. They talked about it in Washington. Roger even got a phone call from the A.C.L.U asking if he wanted their help in the case."

"Who might they be?"

"Oh, that's the American Civil Liberties Union. They're an important organization that sometimes provides legal assistance in cases involving human rights."

"What does all this...commotion signify, friend Dwight?"

"Well, it just means that a lot of people think you got a raw deal losing your farm and they're making a lot of noise to the railroad and other influential people telling them that they'd like to see you get your land back."

"It is a wonderment. Can you make a will?"

"Sure, but wouldn't you want Roger to...?"

"Nay. I had a fancy to make a will. You need not tell Roger."

"O.K. Daniel, I'll stop by tomorrow."

*

Betsy came every day. Daniel was scheduled to be discharged soon but he was very weak. He had barely gotten over the surgery and this episode of septicemia had sapped all of his strength. She suggested that he come with her to Jamaica where he would be able to recuperate away from reporters and the clamor.

"We could stay with my parents. There is room and they'd be very happy to have you as a guest. We could stay for the winter while you get your strength back."

"For the soul of me, dear Betsy, I dare not leave Connecticut. Roger and Dwight may need me." She proposed this idea to Joseph and Roger and, after some discussion, they agreed that it was a good idea to get him to a place where he could recover his health in peace.

"Will you be able to look after him?" Linda asked her. "He's very weak."

"Don't worry. I'll take good care of him."

*

Roger was able to persuade a friend in the New Haven Passport Office to issue a passport to Daniel. They did so with the stipulation that the year of his birth should be shown as 1962. Joseph and Linda drove Daniel and Betsy to the airport.

"Take it easy," they counseled Daniel. "Get plenty of rest. Be careful of sunburn. And keep in touch."

"Farewell, my dear friends," he said. He turned and waved and then followed Betsy into the terminal. At the entrance, he turned and waved. He would never see them again.

CHAPTER 25

Negril, Jamaica.

The big jet swooped low over the turquoise waters of the Caribbean, touched down with a thump on the hot runway of Montego Bay and lumbered to the ramp. The doors opened to admit warm tropical air into the chill cabin atmosphere. After his excitement at takeoff, Daniel slept during most of the flight with his head resting heavily on Betsy's shoulder. Betsy insisted on obtaining a wheelchair for him and quickly guided him through immigration and customs. The main terminal was filled with noisy, eager relatives and friends of the arriving passengers. Betsy recognized an older man among them and rushed over to embrace him.

"Hi, Daddy! How are you? Daddy, this is Daniel," she sang enthusiastically. "Daniel, this is my father, Samuel"

Daniel was momentarily surprised; he didn't expect Betsy's father to be a black man. He rose from the wheelchair and shook the man's hand.

"I am pleased to make your acquaintance, sir,"

Her father was amused by Daniel's reaction. He gave him a broad smile and shook his hand.

"It's good to meet you, man. Can you walk to the car?" He picked up their suitcases and led the way from the terminal to an ancient Volkswagen Beetle.

The drive to Negril wound along the shore with spectacular views of beaches and the sea. They passed through small villages with houses painted in bright pastel shades, garnished with scrawny chickens in the road that barely avoided being run over. Children waved at the car and Samuel honked back.

They arrived after an hour and a half. The house was small and white, set back from the road by a garden enclosed by a low wall of coral blocks. A brilliant fuchsia Bougainvillea partially covered the front of the house and a few chickens rummaged around the door. The air was warm and smelled of the sea and spices. Betsy's mother, a diminutive Chinese woman with a shy smile, came to the doorway to greet them.

"Hi, Mommy!" Betsy called, and ran to hug her and to introduce Daniel. She took Daniel's arm and brought him inside to a large room with an adjoining kitchen and two bedrooms in the back separated by a bathroom. She steered Daniel to one of the bedrooms.

"This is my...our room," she announced. Samuel had placed their luggage on the two twin beds. Daniel was somewhat confused by the sleeping arrangements but they appeared to be acceptable to Betsy's parents. She walked Daniel around outside to a large vegetable garden behind the house where a goat was tethered. The house was close to the beach where a small sailboat lay on the sand. They stood together and watched the sun drop into the sea. It quickly became dark. Daniel had never seen such a magnificent sunset or so many stars.

Dinner was curried goat with a green vegetable that Betsy identified.

"It's callaloo," she told Daniel. "Try it. It's good." Reggae music came from a radio. Daniel enjoyed the food but he was getting very tired. He began to yawn repeatedly.

"You must be exhausted," Betsy said. He nodded. She led him to the bedroom and showed him the bed he was to use. He was asleep within minutes. He dreamed that he was on his farm in Guilford with Elizabeth. She was showing him her vegetable garden.

When Daniel awoke, Betsy was already up. She brought him a delicious breakfast of orange juice, eggs, and coffee, accompanied by fresh bread, honey and pieces of banana, pineapple, mango and papaya.

*

The days flew by and became weeks. Daniel spent much of his time sitting in the sun on the beach, looking at the sea and watching the gulls and pelicans. He dozed in the mornings and napped in the afternoons. He invariably preceeded Betsy to bed and was asleep when she retired.

Betsy's mother, Jackie, worked in a nearby bakery that sold bread and meat patties. Samuel worked in the garden raising the vegetables that he sold or he went out in the sailboat to fish. Samuel Abrahams was sixty-something, erect and in apparent good health and good humor. After working many years at the Reynolds bauxite plant in St. Ann's Bay, he retired to Negril where he and his wife supplemented his pension by selling produce.

Betsy coaxed Daniel to swim with her in the clear, warm water. Daniel wore a pair of swimming trunks borrowed from Samuel. They were too large and he almost lost them. Betsy laughed.

"We'll get a pair for you the next time we go into Negril," she told him.

As the weeks went by, Daniel grew stronger. He began to work in the garden every day. Samuel grew tomatoes, yams, Irish potatoes, dasheen, callaloo, scallions, thyme, sweet peppers and the fiery Scotch bonnet peppers. Daniel cultivated around the rows, weeded, fertilized and removed bugs from the vegetables that the chickens had missed. He accompanied Samuel when he fished and he learned how to raise and lower the sail, to use the tiller and control the jib and when and how to tack. He became tanned and his hair bleached lighter. He was very content.

*

August 6th was Jamaican Independence Day. Daniel and Betsy spent a hot day in Negril walking around the fair. The crowd was lively, innumerable stands offered meat patties and other local delicacies and several bands played reggae music in the Bob Marley style. Betsy took three rides on the merry-go-round, each time failing to get Daniel to join her.

In the evening they returned home. They were alone; Samuel and Jackie remained in Negril for the festivities. Betsy made a pitcher of pineapple and lime juices fortified with dark Jamaican rum. She and Daniel sat on the beach to watch the fireworks and enjoy the cool breeze from the sea. There was no moon but the sky was bright with stars. The pitcher was soon emptied. They sat quietly for a time. Daniel got up and stretched.

"Ah, this has been a lovely day. I would fain stay here with you but I am well-nigh asleep." He walked back to the house, undressed and fell on his bed. He was asleep in minutes.

He had not been sleeping long when he was awakened by Betsy's whisper.

"Daniel, move over." He opened his eyes. Betsy was standing by his bedside. The moon had risen and by its light he could see she was wearing a short nightgown that came to mid-thigh; the thin fabric contoured her nipples.

"What...Betsy, you should not..."

She lay down along side of him, forcing him to give her some space. Her head rested on his outstretched arm. He smelled the musky-spicy scent of her hair. She turned towards him and kissed him, her tongue forcing his lips apart.

"Betsy, you...we must not...," he gasped.

"Shush, just lie back and relax." She rolled on top of him. He felt her small, firm breasts against his chest. His hand began to explore and caress her back and her firm bottom.

"Betsy..."

She straddled him, found the confirmation of his rising passion and engulfed him.

"Betsy...Betsy...Ah, sweet Betsy..."

CHAPTER 26

When Daniel awoke, the sun was high in the sky. Betsy was gone. Her bed had not been slept in. He thought of the previous night with a confused mixture of guilt and pleasure. Betsy came in, smiling, with a breakfast tray. She kissed him on his mouth.

"Did you sleep well?"

"Truly, I slept very well. Methinks too well. I have well-nigh slept the day away."

"Today is Saturday. Would you like to come with me for a drive? I need to buy some things in Montego Bay. We could stay and see a movie."

They drove leisurely along the coast, stopping to view scenes of sea and sky. They spent hours walking barefoot through the water's edge on empty beaches, Betsy's arm around his waist, his around her shoulder. Daniel felt he should say something about their lovemaking of the previous evening.

"About last night," he started, but Betsy placed her fingers across his lips, smiled and shook her head.

What have I...we done? This lovely girl...I desire her. Is that wrong? Elizabeth never had such passion. She cannot be my sister. She is my dear friend. I love her. I feel so close to her. I want her...

They stopped for lunch in a tiny café in Port Chapham. Betsy had been there before and the owner, a smiling black lady, remembered her.

"Good to see you again," she enthused. "How are you? Where you been keepin' yourself?"

"So so, Helen. I've been away to school in the States but I'm home now." Helen took their orders and left for the kitchen.

A young black man sat at an adjoining table. He wore several necklaces and earrings and his hair was long and tied into many long, thin braids. He sat, sullenly nursing a beer. The cigarette he was smoking had a peculiar, pungent odor.

"That's pot...ganja, he's smoking," Betsy whispered. "He's a Rastafarian."

"I know of pot," Daniel told her quietly, "it is bad. What is a Rastafarian?"

Before Betsy could answer, the young man abruptly got up, strode to their table carrying his beer bottle and sat down opposite Daniel. He glowered at them.

"Hey Mon, weh yuh name?" he demanded.

"I'm Daniel Rowland of Guilford, Connecticut. What is *your* name, sir?"

"Jah Roy. Weh you a do yah?"

Daniel looked to Betsy, not understanding.

"He wants to know what you are doing here."

"Why, sir, I am not disposed to discuss that with you," Daniel told him.

Jah Roy looked baffled.

"He says it's none of your business," Betsy interpreted.

"Furthermore, sir, you should not be smoking pot. Of a certainty it is evil."

Jah Roy stared at Daniel in amazement. He responded with a stream of invective.

"He is saying that *you* are evil," Betsy said, "and that you have no business to be here in Jamaica. He says that ganja is sacred and was given by God."

"Ask the scoundrel why I am evil."

"He says because you are white. That the whites have always kept the blacks in slavery. He rejects the white man's world of greed and dishonesty. He says that the blacks are the superior race and that they will take revenge on the whites. The blacks will all return to Africa and form a great country and destroy all the whites. He says..."

"Ask him if he is a Christian."

Jah Roy responded disdainfully in his language.

"He says white Christians lie. God is black and came to Earth as Haile Selassie, the Emperor of Ethiopia."

Helen returned with their lunch. She was upset to see Jah Roy at their table.

"Who invited you here?" she demanded. "Go back to your table!"

Jah Roy got up, glared at Betsy and Daniel, and walked out of the café.

"Enough of that knave," Daniel muttered.

After finishing their lunch, Betsy and Daniel strolled around the small village. The houses and gardens were small but neatly kept. Most of the houses had TV antennas and music came from some open windows. A group of children were playing nearby, skipping rope and chanting a game.

"This place reminds me of Guilford, my Guilford," Daniel remarked. "It is quiet and peaceful, and the people seem to be friendly to each other. Indeed, I see little of the modern conveniences."

"Oh you're wrong, Daniel. These people have telephones, washing machines, TV's, cars, all those things. They get pretty good medical care. There is a dentist. Their kids get their shots and go to school."

"For the soul of me, I would not have thought it. Life here seems simpler, unhurried." They drove on towards Montego Bay.

Ah forsooth, Daniel thought, things are not so simple as I imagined them to be. These folk buy their food in a market and their garments come from a shop yet they are not rushing around constantly seeking news and entertainment, sex and violence. There are always some bad ones like that Jah Roy but most seem good. The people here seem happy and content with their lot. They have time to care for each other. I was wont to think that those machines that make their lives so easy are the cause of many problems. These modern marvels can do much good.

*

Daniel sat in the stern of the small sailboat and handled the tiller. He turned the boat to ride ride easily over the wake of a large powerboat.

"Hey Mon," Samuel told him. "You getting to be a pretty good sailor." Daniel smiled.

"Now truly, Samuel, I have had the best of teachers in you and Betsy."

Samuel turned to attend his hand line and hauled in a large grouper.

"Dis fish will make us a fine dinner tonight. My Jackie'll season him up good with pepper and lime and I'll cook him on the barbecue. Betsy loves fish cooked that way." He bent to gut and scale the fish. "You and my Betsy has gotten real tight these past months," he went on. "You fixin' to stay around a while?"

"Betsy is very dear to me..." Daniel stammered, embarrassed.

"She loves you, Mon. You both welcome to stay as long as you want. Jes' rope in an' enjoy."

*

The letter from the court arrived in Roger's office. Judge Johnson wrote: As stated in Section 52-575, Chapter 926, Title 52 of the Connecticut General Statutes, the statute of limitations to civil actions in cases involving land disputes is fifteen years. The case here exceeds that by one hundred years. Defendant's motion for dismissal is granted. It is so ordered that this case be dismissed.

Roger phoned Dwight with the bad news.

"Is there anything else we can do? Can we appeal Johnson's decision?"

"We could file an appeal with the Connecticut Supreme Court but it's a waste of time because there's no basis. They would uphold Johnson's ruling. I'm afraid Daniel is out of luck. Will you tell him or should I?"

"He's in Jamaica." Dwight said.

"Oh yeah. Well, there's no rush to tell him the bad news. I'll call him."

CHAPTER 27

Daniel awoke very early and dressed. He glanced at Betsy, asleep in her bed, her small form almost child-like. She lay on her side with her legs drawn up, both hands on the pillow near her face. Her lips were slightly parted and there were faint beads of perspiration on her face. He was tempted to bend and kiss her but he didn't want to disturb her. He tiptoed out of the house and walked to the beach. The sun was not yet up and the sky was a pale violet-blue. The Jamaican night wind that blows from the land out to sea had mostly died down. He went to the water's edge. The tide was out and he walked in water that was only inches deep.

It's almost like walking on water, he thought. The bible says that Jesus walked on the water but Jesus came with a message for men. I have no message. I don't know how I came to be here, or why. I have come to think that men are much the same here as in my Guilford. Here on this island the folk seem friendlier...

A loud splashing further offshore interrupted his musings. He walked toward the spot, the water growing slightly deeper as he went further out. As he approached the source of the splashing, he saw that it was a large creature of some kind that was thrashing about. It was a dolphin! He recognized it from the *Flipper* TV shows he had watched. As he grew closer, the dolphin raised its head out of the water and emitted a series of high-pitched beeping sounds. Daniel sensed that the large animal was in distress. He looked for a wound. Then he saw the source of the animal's torment. The dolphin was entangled in a fish net and was resting on the sand in the knee-deep water, too shallow for it to swim clear of the net.

He tried to free it. He had to somehow lift the huge creature in order to pull the net out from under it. The animal seemed to understand that he was trying to help and ceased thrashing but

Daniel couldn't move it. He tried for about fifteen minutes and he was becoming fatigued by the effort. He needed help.

A man was walking on the beach and Daniel called to him. "Help! I need help."

The man rushed into the water toward Daniel. As he came closer, Daniel saw that it was Jah Roy, the Rastafarian from the café.

"Wah, Mon...?"

"It's a dolphin." Daniel shouted. "It is caught in a fish net. Help me to lift him or roll him over" Jah Roy rushed over to Daniel. Together they strained at the task. The tide was coming in and the water grew a little deeper which helped as the dolphin became more buoyant. Finally, with one concerted push, the dolphin rolled over enough so that they were able to pull the net away. The dolphin leaped into the air and sped out to sea. A group of other dolphins jumped high out of the water as if celebrating the return of their comrade and then disappeared.

Both men stared after them for a few moments and then started to walk back to the beach. Daniel was exhausted. He staggered and fell, unable to get up. Jah Roy helped him to his feet and supported him until they reached the land.

"Thank you," Daniel gasped.

Jah Roy glared at him and began to talk very aggressively in his dialect. Daniel did not understand anything he was saying. Jah Roy stood close to Daniel and began to jab him in the chest with his finger as he spoke, forcing Daniel to back up. Jah Roy's voice rose to shouting and he continued to push Daniel backward. He spat in Daniel's face.

"You bastard!" Daniel screamed.

He struck the black man a single hard blow in the chest with his fist. Jah Roy doubled up, gasping, and fell to the ground. He gasped a few times, shuddered and then lay still. Daniel watched him for a minute. He did not seem to be breathing. Daniel knelt by him and put his ear to Jah Roy's chest. He could not hear a heart beat. Jah Roy lay on his back with his eyes open. He was dead.

Daniel began to shake as he knelt by the body.

I have killed him. What should I do now? I did not mean to kill him. I did not want to kill him. He should not have spat in my face. I have killed a man. I am a murderer. I shall be hanged. I can run away and pretend that I had nothing to do with his death...that I just discovered his body. Mayhap I can bury him here in the sand.

He looked around nervously. There was no one in sight.

Nay, I cannot. Someone will come and see me. I do not know what to do.

Daniel stood up. His legs were shaking so much that they barely supported him. He walked back to the house.

*

Samuel phoned the police after he covered the body with a sheet. A constable arrived after half an hour, inspected the body and called for an ambulance. A small group of neighbors gathered on the beach and stare at the covered corps until the ambulance arrived and it was taken away.

"Who are you?" the constable asked Daniel.

"He is our guest." Betsy told him. "He lives here with us."

"Do you have some identification?" Daniel went into the bedroom and produced his passport.

"Who found the body?" the constable asked.

"I found him...it, sir" Daniel said.

"How did you do that?"

"I was walking along the beach..."

"What time was that?"

"It was early in the morning. I do not know the hour."

"Did any of you know this man?"

"His name was Jah Roy. Mr. Rowland and I met him once, a few weeks ago in Port Chapham." Betsy explained.

"What were the circumstances of that meeting?"

"He came over to our table in the restaurant and started an argument with us. He was a Rastafarian. I think he was stoned." Betsy said.

"There will have to be an inquest." The constable said. "I will hold your passport for now at police headquarters in Montego Bay. It will be returned to you later" he told Daniel. "None of you may leave this area until this matter is settled," the constable announced before he drove away.

Jackie left to go to her bakery. Daniel, Betsy and Samuel sat down at the table. Daniel began to shake again.

"You are white as a ghost, mon," Samuel said. "You better have a drink." He poured some rum into a glass for Daniel and drank some himself. "What happened?" Daniel coughed once as he downed the liquor.

"I killed him," he whispered. "He spat in my face and I hit him." Daniel related what happened. "I did not mean to kill him. I struck him only once but he fell and died."

"What did you hit him with?" Samuel asked. "I didn't see no marks on him."

"I struck him in the belly with my fist. I did not mean to kill him. I did not want to kill him." Daniel cried. "What am I to do?"

"Shush," Betsy said. "We'll just have to wait and see what happens."

CHAPTER 28

"It's Mr. Bush on the phone." Roger's secretary announced.

"Hello, Mr. Bush. Congratulations on your victory. What can I do for you?"

"Our victory is a hollow one, Mr. Rowland. Someone wrote a letter to Ann Landers about this case and she printed it in her column. Derogatory letters have been pouring in to Amtrak and the Transit Authority. Hasn't affected ridership, of course, but there's been some graffiti and generally bad feelings toward the railroad. We have a proposal that we think would benefit your client as well as the railroad, the Authority and Clinton."

"I'd like to hear it," Roger said.

"Clinton would divide the property into two parts, a ten acre portion that contains the railroad right of way, the firing range and the dump; and an unused eight acre portion. The Town of Clinton would revise their eminent domain condemnation proceedings to the ten-acre parcel, pay your client for it and recognize his ownership of the remaining eight acres."

"How much would Clinton pay?"

"Ten thousand, but there's more."

"I'm listening," Roger told him.

"Amtrak and the Transit Authority are prepared to pay your client a total one-time payment of forty thousand for, let's say, past use of the property."

"Well, fifty thousand dollars is a lot less than three million but we're not in a position to haggle. What do you guys get? The quid pro quo?"

"All we want is some favorable PR to make everyone happy. A few newspaper stories, that kind of stuff. What do you think?"

"We accept." Roger said. "Send me the papers."

Roger lost no time in telephoning the news to Daniel.

"We lost the battle," he told him, "but we won the war. You have eight acres and fifty thousand dollars. Is that O.K.?"

"It is indeed, Roger. "I am most grateful to you and to Dwight."

*

Daniel was dreaming. He was making love to Betsy. She was naked and lay on her back with her head resting in the crook of his arm. He was kissing her and fondling her breasts. He bent to kiss her erect nipples.

"Oh Daniel," she whispered. Her voice sounded different. He looked up to find it was Elizabeth in his arms. She faded and he found himself on the beach on Leete's Island in Guilford. Jah Roy appeared and began hitting Daniel with a stick. Daniel parried the blows with his arms. Jah Roy shoved a gun at him and screamed, "Shut up, you bastard!" Daniel struck him a blow that knocked him down. Jah Roy was dead. Daniel began to run away along the water's edge. A voice called to him.

"Daniel, Daniel." It was a dolphin. "Beware, Daniel," the dolphin told him. "A calamity at three in the afternoon.."

"What manner of calamity? When? Who am I to warn?"

"Soon," the dolphin said "The innocent ones of Port Royal." The dolphin leaped high into the air and swam away.

Daniel awoke. He was trembling and covered with sweat although the night air was cool. He lay awake until daybreak. In the morning he told Betsy and Samuel the latter part of his dream.

"Where is Port Royal?" Daniel asked them.

"It's a town just across the harbor from Kingston. It's on the other side of the island. Why?"

"Something dreadful will happen there. I know it."

"A calamity?" Samuel said. "Other than hurricanes, the last calamity we had was the big earthquake in Kingston back in 1907. There were big landslides that destroyed most of the town."

"It was just a dream, Daniel," Betsy said. "Forget it.

*

The inquest on Jah Roy's death was held in Montego Bay. A magistrate presided over the small group. Daniel, Betsy, Samuel and Jackie were notified to attend. Several Rastafarians were also present. The magistrate read the autopsy report.

"Examination of the deceased's remains failed to reveal any evidence of foul play. There were no wounds or bruises on the body and the internal organs were intact and appeared normal. Death is presumed to have occurred as a result of cardiac arrest from natural causes." The magistrate looked up.

"If there are no objections, this hearing is closed."

A constable motioned Daniel to follow him to the adjoining police station.

"Here is your passport back, Mr. Rowland. You are free to come and go as you choose. By the way, we read about your good fortune in the American newspaper. Congratulations."

*

The marijuana started its journey from a warehouse near Cali, in Colombia. The shipment was a large one with a street value well over one million dollars. Heavily armed men drove the dried plants by night through the jungles of Panama to the coast of Nicaragua where a boat waited. The *Oro Blanca* was a "go-fast," a type of boat favored by drug runners. Manufactured by Edward Dondo in Columbia, she was thirty-five feet long with an open hull and capable of speeds of fifty knots. In addition to the stacks of the large, sealed plastic packages of marijuana, she carried 50-gallon drums of fuel that would extend her range to Jamaica.

The crew of three swarthy Nicaraguans was well paid for their work. They were tough sailors who would not hesitate to cut a throat. The *Oro Blanca* would carry the marijuana to Port Royal, where a Jamaican would be waiting to arrange the transport of the cargo to nearby *Norman Manley Airport*. Local police officials were bribed to look the other way and to facilitate the transfer. A small aircraft would carry the marijuana to a landing strip in Florida after refueling at a remote out island in the Bahamas. It was all arranged.

CHAPTER 29

Daniel remained troubled. He felt guilty about Jah Roy's death. He wanted to confess his responsibility at the inquest but Betsy convinced him to remain silent. He was also disturbed by his dream and when Betsy suggested a possible trip to Kingston, he immediately agreed to go.

"It's the Terra Nova Heritage Food Festival we have every year," she explained. "It featuring Jamaican food and cooking. It'll be fun and we can visit Port Royal. Daddy can drive us to the train station in Montego Bay."

The train to Kingston was old but comfortable. Almost every seat was occupied. There were many families and children, some of whom played and raced up and down the aisle, making it seem like a large group on an outing. Daniel watched the scenery and dozed; Betsy read. Jackie had prepared a picnic lunch for them with sandwiches and bottles of Red Stripe beer. After five hours the train arrived in Kingston. Daniel and Betsy found a room in a hotel near the train station and spent a quiet night.

*

The *Oro Blanca* tied up at the small pier in Port Royal. She had burned up most of the fuel during the trip and the metal drums were thrown overboard as they were emptied. Only the large piles of marijuana packages remained, covered with a green tarp.

Adolfo, the "captain," asked, "What was the name of the guy who was supposed to meet us?"

"Jah Roy," one of the others told him. "Crazy name."

Adolfo went ashore to find a phone. He returned to the boat fifteen minutes later.

"No answer," he reported. "We'll wait."

*

The next day Daniel and Betsy walked to the Craft Market where the festival was in progress. It was the final day of the event. Some of the exhibits were being dismantled but there were still many that displayed typical Jamaican dishes and offered a taste. They strolled around for three hours admiring the exhibits, chatting with the participants, and sampling many of the dishes and ingredients.

"I'm hungry," Betsy announced. "All these tiny tastes gave me an appetite. Let's find a restaurant."

They were enjoying a dish of highly spiced jerk pork when Betsy's attention was drawn to a diner at an adjoining table. The man was obviously in distress; he dropped his utensils to the floor, threw his head back, clutched his throat and tried to stand up. He was choking!

Betsy leaped to her feet, knocking her chair over, and rushed over to the man. She approached him from behind, wrapped her arms around his chest, locked her hands together and gave several hard thrusts. A piece of meat burst from his mouth and he was able to breath. He sank back to his chair, relieved.

"Thank you," he gasped after a few moments. "You really saved me. I could have choked to death. Are you a doctor or a nurse?"

"No," Betsy told him, "they teach that to everyone in the States." She returned to her table. Daniel was staring in amazement.

"How did...what did you do?"

"It's called the Heimlich Maneuver, to help someone who's choking," she explained. "Almost everybody knows how to do it."

The man, a tall, light-colored Jamaican in his sixties, now fully recovered, came over to their table and introduced himself.

"My name is Albert Phillips and I am very grateful to you, young lady. You probably saved my life."

Betsy introduced herself and Daniel.

"We're just visiting for the food fair," she said. "And we want to see Port Royal."

Phillips smiled. "You picked the right man to save. I happen to be the curator of the Fort Charles Maritime Museum in Port Royal and it would be my pleasure to show you around. It's the least I can do to show my gratitude. I won't take 'no' for an answer."

Phillips insisted on paying for their lunch and led them to his car.

"You can reach Port Royal by the ferry from West Beach Dock or the Victoria Pier over on Ocean Boulevard, but we'll drive around on the Palisadoes Road."

Port Royal was situated near the end of a narrow sand peninsula that curved around from the mainland enclosing Kingston Harbor.

As they drove along, Phillips commented, "Port Royal once had the reputation of being the wickedest city on earth. Pirates like Blackbeard and Henry Morgan used to come here and their crews roamed through the streets and grog shops, carousing and looting but that all came to an end when the town was destroyed in 1692."

"What happened?" Betsy asked.

"An earthquake. On June seventh, at eleven forty-three in the morning. It lasted three minutes. Houses toppled over, the ground opened up and 'swallowed' people, and then a huge tidal wave came and swept over the town. There was nothing left."

"Have there been other earthquakes here?" Betsy asked him.

"Yes indeed. Kingston was almost completely devastated by one in 1907. There were bad landslides. It was like Sodom and Gomorrah." Phillips stopped in front of an old church.

"This is St. Peter's," he told them. "Some of the silver that Henry Morgan looted from the cathedral in Panama, is stored inside. The place is always locked but I can arrange a visit if you are interested. There's a graveyard in the back with the tomb of Lewis Galdy. He was a Frenchman who was swallowed up during the earthquake and then thrown back up."

"My word!" Daniel said. "He must have been so wicked that even the ground would not have him." They drove on and came to another old structure.

"Fort Charles," Phillips announced. "Built in 1656. "There were originally six forts but this is the only one left. Admiral Lord Nelson commanded this fort in 1779."

"Yes," Daniel said. "I recall our schoolmaster telling us something about it." Phillips gave Daniel a peculiar look to see if he was joking. They continued on.

"And here's my Maritime Museum. It used to be the headquarters of the British Navy in the Caribbean. Lord Nelson was here. We have lots of model ships inside. We can stop in later. They drove past the airport, through the small, ramshackle town and stopped in front of a low building near the beach.

"Morgan's Harbor Beach Club." Phillips told them. "It's almost three o'clock. Why don't we go in and have a beer? Hello, what's this?" He looked at the pier where a boat was moored. It was the *Oro Blanca*. Phillips stared at the boat for a minute.

"That's an Edward Dondo 'go-fast'," he said. "Drug runners use them. I happen to know about boats. They can outrun most of our Coast Guard boats. I wonder what's under that tarp?"

They were about one hundred yards away from the pier. Phillips took a pair of binoculars from a pocket and scanned the boat. One of the plastic bags of marijuana had fallen off the pile and out from under the tarp.

"Ganja!" he shouted. "Pot. They have a huge pile of it." His elbow inadvertently blew the horn.

Adolfo came out on deck. He saw the car.

"Policia!" he shouted. He grabbed an assault rifle and began to fire rapidly at the car. A bullet crashed through the windshield narrowly missing Phillips. They all ducked to the floor. One of the crew frantically untied the mooring lines; the other man tried to start the boat's engines. The *Oro Blanca* began to slowly drift away from the pier making it harder for

Adolfo to shoot accurately but some of his bullets were still hitting the car.

"Get out!" Phillips shouted. When Adolfo briefly stopped firing to reload, they all jumped out of the car and took cover behind it. Adolfo resumed firing at the car. Patrons looked out of the Club door and ducked back in.

The firing alerted a constable across the harbor and there were phone calls from the Club. A few minutes later, a police launch started out from the Kingston shore but it would take at least ten minutes for it to reach the Port Royal side. The crewman on the *Oro Blanca* kept trying to start the engines; the other man began firing at the car with a pistol.

Daniel, Betsy and Phillips lay prone on the sand behind the car. The car's engine was still running and the exhaust fumes were making them all cough. Some of the rounds struck the car with a loud bang, causing them all to flinch; other shots kicked up sand close to them. They were pinned down.

CHAPTER 30

"We cannot remain here," Daniel said. "Those villains are bound to hit us." Moments later, Betsy cried out.

"Oh!" She had been hit. Daniel scooped her into his arms, stood up and began to run towards the door of the Club. Adolfo switched his weapon to full automatic and fired at Daniel. The hail of bullets kicked up sand close behind him but he made the entrance safely. Inside, eight patrons lay on the floor, sheltering themselves from the gunfire.

"Help us, please!" Daniel yelled. "She's been wounded." He laid Betsy gently on the floor. Her blouse was soaked with blood.

"My arm," she cried. The bullet had made a deep gouge in the fleshy part of her upper arm and the wound was bleeding profusely. On of the customers crawled over and offered a clean handkerchief which Daniel placed over the wound.

At that moment a sharp jolt shook the building and the floor began to roll. The building trembled and there was a loud rumbling sound.

"My God, an earthquake!" one of the patrons shouted. Women screamed in terror, men yelled. Daniel lifted Betsy and carried her out through a side door. This is the calamity that the dolphin warned about in my dream. He placed Betsy on the sand and glanced toward the pier. The shooting had stopped. He rushed back into the Club to find some of the patrons shrieking and milling about in confusion.

"Go outside!" he commanded. One of the women fainted; Daniel half-carried, half-dragged her outside. He returned inside to guide the remaining patrons out. Seconds later the building collapsed to a pile of rubble.

In the harbor, the water rapidly drained away and the *Oro Blanca* rested briefly on the bottom before a huge tidal wave appeared, forty feet high, engulfed the boat and rushed up over the beach. It was over in less than a minute.

The *Oro Blanca* and her crew were gone. The pier was gone. The police launch was gone but men bobbed about in life jackets where the launch had been. A few plastic packages of marijuana came to the surface. Phillips' car lay on its side draining water. Phillips still clung to it, drenched but unscathed.

*

An ambulance carried Betsy and Daniel to a clinic in Kingston. It was a long ride because the road had been damaged by the quake and the ambulance had to carefully detour around many large cracks in the roadway. Buildings had collapsed in Port Royal and there were some injured people but no fatalities.

A doctor closed Betsy's wound with sutures, gave her a tetanus shot and some pain medication. She and Daniel returned to their hotel. Daniel insisted that Betsy rest in bed for the next few days. He brought her meals and wanted to feed her until she protested that, it was her left arm that was wounded, thank you very much, and she could manage. They phoned Samuel to meet them and took the train back to Montego Bay.

The American newspapers reported the earthquake as a relatively mild one with little damage and few injuries; three point five on the Richter Scale. Joseph phoned and Betsy told him the story of their adventure in Port Royal and reassured him that she and Daniel were O.K.

*

Betsy's wound healed quickly. The local newspaper carried a story of Daniel's heroism during the earthquake. He had a check mailed to Phillips that would provide for a new car. Daniel took long walks on the beach, sometimes with Betsy, often alone and pondered his future.

What should I do now? Remain here with Betsy or return to Connecticut? I could farm my land, build a small house...but I will be alone. Here I have Betsy but these are not my people.

CHAPTER 31

Daniel was working in the garden with Samuel, weeding between rows of peppers. The day was hot and humid and for a time both men worked in silence. Reggae music drifted from a radio in the house. Betsy was shopping in Montego Bay. Samuel paused to drink some water.

"Hey Daniel, what you goin' to do now that you're getting all that money and your land back?" Daniel paused from his weeding.

"I do not rightly know, friend Samuel. I had a fancy to stay here with Betsy and pay you for my lodging and keep but..."

"I can't let you pay us, man. You're family and you're welcome to stay as long as you like. You know my Betsy loves you, man."

"And I love her. But I must return to claim the land for my family." Samuel thought for a moment.

"Why did you come here, man?" he asked quietly.

"Betsy brought me here, she wanted me to come."

"No, man, I don't mean here to Jamaica. I mean from your time?"

"For the soul of me, I do not know. I have thought on it many an hour. I surely did not will it. I was a happy man with a good wife and a baby coming..."

"Maybe something...someone...God, sent you here to us?"

"But why? Why me? I was a simple farmer.

"Jesus was a simple carpenter," Samuel replied. Daniel was shocked.

"Jesus came to save mankind, to tell of God's grace. I have nothing to tell."

"Maybe He just wanted you to tell us that all our modern stuff is distracting us from the basic things like, you know, love. Jackie and me heard you talking to Betsy about that."

Daniel nodded. They worked together in silence for another hour. The day grew warmer.

"Samuel, I would like to go for a sail. May I borrow the boat?"

"Sure man, I'll help you get her out." They walked to the beach and pushed the boat out until it floated. Samuel held the boat while Daniel waded out and climbed aboard, lowered the rudder into the water and raised the sail.

"You want me to come with you?"

"Nay, I would fain go alone. I will return soon."

There was a light breeze and the boat moved out smartly. Daniel steered away from the shore. The sea was calm with gentle swells and the land was soon out of sight. He sailed for an hour, maintaining a straight course with the tiller.

He was startled by a splash near the boat and saw that a dolphin appeared very close and was swimming along with the boat. He was able to reach out and pat the large creature. Could this be the same one that Jah Roy and I rescued? If so, he is more fortunate than I am...we were both trapped away from our natural places but he was able to return while I remain a prisoner in this time.

"I wish you a good life, Master dolphin," he said.

Daniel noticed that it was growing foggy; he was sailing into a fog bank. He tacked to remain in the clear but he was soon engulfed. This is almost like the cloud that brought me here, he thought. I am not worried. I shall just come about and steer straight and I shall soon reach the shore.

CHAPTER 32

Betsy returned from her shopping trip in the late afternoon. She became alarmed when Samuel told her that Daniel was out sailing.

"How long has he been gone, Daddy?"

"About five hours."

"That's a long time." She went down to the beach and looked out to sea. It was very hazy and there were no boats in sight.

"I'm worried Daddy. He has no sailing experience."

"Don't worry. He's a good sailor. I taught him. He'll be back soon."

But as the day faded into dusk and evening Daniel had not returned. Betsy phoned the police in Negril. They referred her to the Harbor Police, but there was no answer there. It was now dark. She called the Coast Guard in Montego Bay. They asked if there were lights aboard the boat.

"No lights," she told them.

"It's too dark to search tonight. Give us a call in the morning if he's still not back. Not to worry, the sea is calm and no heavy weather is predicted."

Betsy spent a miserable, sleepless night. At first light she went down to the beach, hoping against hope to see him. She strained her eyes searching the horizon for any sign of a boat. There was none. She called the Coast Guard again.

"We'll send a boat out to look."

The day dragged by without a phone call. Towards evening Betsy was frantic and phoned the Coast Guard again.

"We searched all day," they told her "but we didn't find him. We're going to send out an aircraft tomorrow."

But heavy thunderstorms and high winds the next two days forestalled the launching of the search planes. On the third day an airplane was sent out. The air search continued two more days. The Coast Guard called Betsy.

"We're dreadfully sorry, Miss, but we're going to have to call off the search. There's no sign of him or the boat."

"Isn't it possible that he put in on some deserted beach or cove?" she pleaded.

"We checked the coast for many miles in each direction. If he had landed we would have seen the boat. Sorry, Miss."

*

The phone call came in the early evening.

"Dr. Pellegrini, it's Betsy...in Jamaica." She was sobbing.

"What's wrong, Betsy?"

"It's Daniel. He's...gone."

"Gone? How?"

"He went sailing in our little boat. He's done it before. My father showed him how and said he was a good sailor. But he's disappeared."

"Was he alone?"

"Yes." She was crying so hard that Joseph had trouble understanding her.

"How long has he been gone?"

"Seven days. They searched all over for four days but there's no trace of him.

"My God! Betsy, I'm so sorry. Is there anything I...we can do?"

"No," she sobbed. "Nothing."

"Would you like to come and stay with us for a while?"

"Maybe. I'll see. Thank you."

"Please keep in touch with us," Joseph said before he hung up.

"What is it?" Linda asked. She saw the expression of pain and sorrow on his face.

"It's Daniel. He disappeared in a small boat. They searched for him for four days but they didn't find him or the boat."

“Oh, Joe,” she said, her eyes filling with tears. “Is he really...gone? It’s hard to believe it. How is Betsy taking it? I think she was in love with him.”

“She sounded very distraught...a wreck.”

CHAPTER 33

Four months later.

Joseph answered the phone.

"It's Dwight. Can Roger and I come over tomorrow? Betsy is flying in and I'd like to bring Karen."

Everyone arrived at the Pellegrini's the next evening. Linda and Joseph hugged Betsy in welcome. They all sat around the living room. Dwight cleared his throat.

"When Daniel was in the hospital, he asked me to help him make a will. Even a second year law student can do that. I want to read it to you. I'll skip the 'being of sound mind' legal stuff. As you know, his total assets were in excess of sixty thousand dollars. There will be taxes, of course, but basically he left one-third of his estate to Roger; one-third to Joseph, Linda and the children; and one-third to Betsy and her family. He also left generous amounts to Karen and to me." He paused for a moment.

"He also left his farm to Roger. He would have liked to farm it himself. He had this idea of farming it the way it was done in his time, you know, the same crops, same methods and so on. He thought that people might be interested and come to visit. A kind of living museum of Colonial days."

"That was a splendid idea," Roger sad, "but now that Daniel is gone..." Everyone was silent.

"Couldn't we find someone, like hire someone to do that, you know, what Daniel wanted to do?" Nick asked.

"That's a good idea, Nick" Dwight said. "We can try to find someone."

Linda put her arm around Betsy's shoulder.

"You know," she said to everyone. "Daniel wanted to retain his farm and with Roger and Dwight's help, he got it back. Daniel showed us the importance of simple values; honesty, friendship, family. He left us richer in more than just the money.

The farm can be a memorial to him." They all nodded in agreement.

Linda invited them all to share a simple buffet. The mood was happy. Each recounted episodes they had with Daniel, some of them funny. There was laughter and good spirits. It was an impromptu memorial service to him.

After hours of congenial conversation, the visitors embraced, promised to stay in touch and departed.

*

Daniel had been sailing for a long time. The fog became so dense that he could not see the sky or the sea ahead, but he knew that if he held a straight course he would eventually reach a destination. The fog was warm and above it he could just make out the sun. The sea was calm and the breeze was slight but steady as it moved the boat along through the milky haze. He felt very peaceful. A dolphin appeared nearby and spoke to him. Perhaps it was the one he and Jah Roy rescued. The dolphin swam along with the boat. After a long while, Daniel thought he heard someone calling. It was a woman's voice. It sounded familiar. He could not make out the words. It sounded like...yes, it was Elizabeth's voice! His heart beat faster and he sailed in her direction.

Printed in the United States
2301